Christmas Eve, Eve

A SPICY CHRISTMAS NOVELLA

CHRIS REILLY

Christmas Eve, Eve
Copyright © 2024 Chris Reilly

ISBN No: 978-1-0687502-0-5

Cover Design: Chris Reilly Author
www.Depositphotos.com
www.canva.com
© Repixo via Canva.com

Interior Format: Chris Reilly Author

All rights reserved. No portion of this book may be reproduced, copied, distributed in any form without prior written permission from the author, except for brief quotations in the context of a book review.

No part of this book may be used to create, feed, or refine artificial intelligence models, for any purpose, without written permission from the author. The scanning, uploading and distribution of this book without written permission is a theft of the author's intellectual property.

This is a work of fiction, names, characters, businesses, places, events and incidents are either the product of the author's imagination or used to provide authenticity in a fictitious manner. Any resemblance to actual persons, living or dead, or actual events is purely coincidental.

For Nancy,
Your light will shine on, forever in our hearts

Chapter 1

"Eve, tell me you didn't miss the flight."

"Do you seriously think I'm calling to tell you I missed the flight?"

I adjust the rearview mirror on my rental. All around me is white. The interior of the SUV, the exterior, the airport building, the snow. If not for the beautiful cloud-free blue sky, I'd think I'd just walked into a white box.

At least it's not snowing right now, though the six inches I've heard all about since I landed in Wyoming seems like a lot to me. But I'm South Carolina, born and raised. Snow is a novelty to me. When it does snow in Columbia, it barely sticks and lasts maybe half a day.

How do I get this heater to work? Despite my heavy padded coat, thick jumper and fleece lined leggings, it's freezing.

"It wouldn't be the first time," Ashlynn snort laughs.

"I'll have you know I am very organized. I'm in the rental, programming the GPS now."

Ashlynn squeals. My phone has connected to the car's Bluetooth, so her voice echoes all around me. I can't help but smile.

Ashlynn is my favorite person in the entire world. We're cousins, but might as well be sisters. I'm closer to her than I am to my own sister. Which isn't surprising given there is four years' difference between me and Holly. My sister being the eldest.

There is only eleven months' difference between Ashlynn and me. Her dad is my mom's brother. They lived on the next block when we were kids, so we went to the same schools together, right until college, when she went off to Ohio State College of Nursing and I headed north to Duke in North Carolina.

A day never passed where we didn't speak. Every spring break, we would go to Miami together, where we had some wild and crazy adventures.

Ashlynn is as far from the carefree, tits to the wind, party girl she was back then. Now, she's all grown up and civilized. A nurse dating a firefighter, who is a bona fide superhero. His proposal just over a year ago was during a cruise on an island in the Bahamas.

Carter comes from money and has a trust fund. He doesn't dip into it often unless it comes to treating his girl. If I didn't love her so much, I'd be downright jealous and hate her for finding the life she has.

"You're getting married this week," I say, sitting back in the seat as the heater kicks in and warm air blows straight into my face. I adjust the vents, so my eyeballs don't dry out.

"I know. Can you believe it?"

"Not hardly," I laugh. "You swinging from a stripper pole in neon green panties and matching nipple tassels is a memory still implanted in my brain."

"Oh my God, do not bring shit like that up this week," she cries, mortified. "Besides, that was a million years ago. I'm respectable now."

As if I would. It wouldn't matter if I did, not to Carter. He knows all about his fiancé's wild past. And finds it amusing. They're perfect for each other.

"It's forecast to snow again soon, so hurry your ass up and get here, okay? I don't need to be worrying about you driving in the snow."

"I've rented a tank," I laugh. "I think this thing could get me through the Apocalypse."

"Don't underestimate the snow."

"Now you sound like dad."

"Did he send you a You Tube video on how to drive in snowy weather?"

"At least six. My favorite was the one of a blizzard in Antarctica. You gotta be careful in those white outs."

"He cares," she says, with a grin in her voice.

"I wish he was here."

"You know he would be if he could," Ashlynn says.

She stops short of bringing up the divorce. It is the furthest thing from amicable. Both my parents were invited, but mom pulled the 'it's my brother' card. Dad is staying away to keep the peace. He has given me a gift to give to Ashlynn before the ceremony.

"Anyway," she changes the subject, knowing it's a sore spot for me. "Stop arguing with me and get your ass on the road."

"Can't wait to see your face, bitch."

"Or yours, jerk," she replies.

We're both huge Supernatural fans. Bitch and jerk are names the two main characters call each other.

"Tonight is going to be so much fun. Drive safe."

The guests have been invited to a cocktail evening. Not any old cocktail evening. This one involves two professional cocktail makers. They've been hired to teach the wedding guests how to make our own concoctions.

It has beautiful disaster written all over it.

A laugh bursts out of me as I pass the sign for the town where Ashlynn is getting married. I already know about the place. It still makes me chuckle when I think of it. My Christmas obsessed cousin is getting married on Christmas eve, in a town called Noel Ridge. In the middle of a snow-storm.

It's not quite a storm, but it has started to snow while I've been driving. It's not too heavy and the roads have been plowed, so I'm not worried.

The closer I get to Noel Ridge, the more pristine everything looks. Along the way, snowbanks have formed off the side of the road. They were slushy and brown on the road towards the town. Now they're almost postcard perfect.

Whichever way they look, I would not want to end up with my car in one of them.

About five miles back, I figured I'd just go with it and tuned into a radio station playing Christmas tunes. *'Christmas Wrapping'* by the Waitresses is playing now. It's far superior to the cutesy, teeny bopper tunes some of the other stations are playing. Or the heavy hitter ballads, which are even worse.

The GPS lets me know to take the next turn, then I'll reach my destination. There are a lot of trees, but I see the turn and head that way. After another quarter mile, I come upon a sign for the Ridgewood Inn.

Through the falling snow, a building appears ahead of me.

"Wow," I mutter. The building itself is huge, but it is the definition of small-town charm.

The Inn is a two-story structure clad in gray timber. The sloped roof is covered in dark wooden shingles, with exposed wooden beams beneath the eaves. A wide front porch stretches across the front, framed by wooden columns with hanging lanterns that will cast a soft glow in the evening.

It has tall windows overlooking views of the surrounding countryside, or maybe the small town of Noel Ridge. I'll know if the snow ever slows down enough to see what lies beyond the Inn.

Large flower boxes overflowing with seasonal plants line the porch rail. It's exactly how I imagine the place where Ashlynn will get married.

As I turn towards the parking lot, an old truck is blocking the way in. Not idling, it's stopped and perpendicular to the road. Two men are standing by the truck, one on his cell phone, the other looks like he is trying to figure things out.

When the one not on the phone spots my car, he hurries over. I lower the window.

"Sorry ma'am," he says. "The gentleman's vehicle broke down. We're trying to get a local tow truck up here to move it. We'll be digging out a path so cars can pass by if you just give us a few minutes."

"I hope no one was hurt," I say. The truck looks as if it's slid in the snow.

"The driver tried to pull it to the side before it cut out but wasn't successful."

Behind him, two men appear with large snow shovels and the man at the window tells me they'll be as quick as possible. I thank him and close the window.

Just those few minutes have taken all the heat out of the car. Reaching over to the passenger seat, I grab my pink woolly hat and pull it on, turning the heat up again.

The man on the cell phone tips his head back as he talks, looking frustrated. I can't make out his features, but don't think I recognize him. He must be from Carter's side of the family. Ashlynn booked out the entire inn for the wedding.

The men make quick work of the snowdrifts and clear a makeshift path for me to move around the broken-down truck. All my focus is on navigating the narrow pathway, so I don't hit it.

I wave to the man in thanks as he points to the lot and go find a space.

The same man hurries over and helps me with my bags. I follow him up the steps onto the porch and he holds the door open for me.

"Enjoy your stay," he says, then turns back and trots down the stairs before I can thank him or grab my purse to give him a tip.

I'll catch him later. The warmth inside hits me as soon as I cross the threshold. The lobby is as impressive as the exterior, with high ceilings and exposed beams. The floors are polished hardwood, softened by large woven rugs. A massive fireplace dominates one wall, crackling with a fire that adds much needed warmth. There is no one else waiting to be checked in, so I head to the desk.

"Welcome to the Ridgewood Inn. May I take your name, please?"

I give her my information as I tug off my hat. That fireplace really is doing its job. I'm starting to sweat. As she checks the computer, I glance around again. To the left of the reception desk, there is a seating area with rustic wooden furniture, paired with plush armchairs and cozy throws.

An archway leads into what looks to be a bar area. Behind the desk, a hallway goes back to where I presume the stairs are, which leads to the second story.

A huge Christmas tree, beautifully decorated, dominates another corner of the room. It's tall enough to almost hit the ceiling, but there is just enough room for the gorgeous, glowing star.

Halloween has always been my favorite holiday. Ashlynn lives and breathes for Christmas, hence why she's getting married on Christmas Eve.

My attention is drawn to the door opening and a gust of snow coming in. The man with the broken down truck hurries in and closes the door. I move to the side slightly so he can talk to the second receptionist, trying not to stare too obviously.

Chapter 2

This cannot be happening.

The biggest pitch of my life and a goddamn truck is about to ruin everything. I should have flown, but the cost of airline tickets at this time of year is astronomical and way out of my budget. I figured my truck could make it. It managed most of the hundred-and-ten-mile journey.

Then it shit the fucking bed with fifty miles to go.

I'm about to lose my mind. This meeting is everything to me and my company. If I don't make it there at ten in the morning, I'm going to lose my shot. Not to mention the money I've laid out already drawing up the plans. The hours upon hours preparing the pitch. Convincing Henrickson Inc to give me a chance will all be wasted.

And I'll be letting everyone down.

Fucking typical, I manage to get the truck to the only hotel in the area, but it's fully booked out for a wedding. Who gets married at Christmas anyway? Romantic idiots. That's who.

I'm so desperate, I even asked a random woman to give me her room. I don't do shit like that normally. There is nothing normal about this situation. Once I got over the desperation of asking and being shot down, I almost asked if she wouldn't mind sharing.

Letting my cock start calling the shots is only going to make this worse. That woman was stunning. In her pink hat and thick padded coat, blonde hair spilling down her back. Her red lipstick drew my attention to her mouth. Inappropriate things ran through my head in a split second.

That was a moment of madness. I pushed it aside as quickly as it came. I've got more important things to worry about. Trying to force a woman out of a room she has booked and paid for is a dick move.

More guests are arriving. I'm staring at my phone in one hand, and the mug of steaming hot chocolate in the other. Wondering what the hell I'm going to do.

Will they let me sleep on the couch over there? It looks comfortable and with the fireplace, I'm not gonna go cold. The only other option is sleeping in the truck. Unless I want to end up an icicle like Jack Nicholson at the end of The Shining, that is a bad idea.

It's getting to the point I'm going to have to make a call I don't want to. It took a lot of finessing and careful planning to get Henrickson Inc to consider me for the job. How can I fall at the first God damn hurdle? And a stupid one at that.

There has got to be a way for me to pull this off. I shove the phone back in my pocket and walk back to reception to beg for their couch. The woman who came around the corner a few moments ago approaches me before I can.

"Hi, I'm Ashlynn. I heard about what happened with your vehicle and needing a room."

Are all the women here next level hot? It's like adding insult to injury.

"Yeah, I'm in a bit of a predicament."

"I'm sure there is something we can do to help."

"I'm not sure what."

Now that I'm up close and personal, I can confirm I don't know him. Damn, he's good looking. He has to be one of Carter's firefighter friends.

His strong, defined jawline and high cheekbones give him a chiseled, classic look, enhanced by his smooth, olive-toned complexion. His dark hair is thick and slightly tousled, falling just above his ears with a natural wave. It's in disarray from the wind and there are snowflakes slowly melting in it.

His eyes are a beautiful, dark gray color, like steel. Light stubble adds a bit of ruggedness to his appearance.

Damn, he is hot.

"You're all checked in, Miss Dalton. Here is your key, if you could just sign here and here."

My attention is drawn from the hot stranger, not before he turns and catches my eye. Just as quickly, he looks away.

"Do you have any rooms?" he asks.

That's odd. He doesn't have a room already? The receptionist explains there is a wedding here and they're fully booked.

He groans and we all turn to him. "My truck is broken down and the tow can't get here until tomorrow," he says. "I have a room at a hotel in Evergreen Hollow, but it's another fifty miles away."

"I'm really sorry, sir, we just don't have any vacancies."

He thinks for a minute, tapping his hand against the desk. "Are there no guests who could double up, just for one night?"

I snort. I can't help it. I'm not even sure why. Those dark, attractive eyes turn to me, and he studies me with a frown.

"I'm afraid we can't ask our guests to do that, sir. We're hosting a wedding and all the guests have the rooms available."

"There's gotta be something you can do."

"I wish there was. I understand your predicament. I'm sure Anthony is doing everything he can to source help with your vehicle."

He blows out an exasperated sigh. It's not the receptionist's fault his truck broke down. I get it, it's frustrating. I'd be losing my shit if it was me, but what is the woman supposed to do?

"Would you like a complimentary hot chocolate while you wait?" she asks him.

Why am I still standing here? I have *my* room key. I need to let Ashlynn know I'm here. I'm dying to see her.

"What about you? Are you alone?"

My head whips back to the stranger. "I'm sorry, me?" I point to myself.

"Yeah. Are you alone?"

"That's none of your business."

"All I mean is," he turns to face me. "Can't you bunk with one of the other guests?"

"Sir, you can't ask our guests to switch rooms."

"What she said," I tell him.

"Come on, help a guy out."

My room is my room. If I wanted to share, I wouldn't have told Ashlynn to ensure I got my own space. I get he's in a tough spot, but it's not my problem to fix.

"Sorry, I can't help you."

I gather up my things and turn away. My receptionist gives me directions. The man huffs behind me but doesn't argue with me. I hear him telling the woman he will take that hot chocolate.

As I round the corner, I almost bump straight into Ashlynn.

"Eve!" she screams and pulls me into a hug. "I am so happy to see you," she squeezes me tighter. "I need a drink," she says into my ear. "Carter's mom is driving me crazy."

"She's still trying to take over?"

"Not to me. Carter knocked that on the head, but I caught her with the catering staff trying to change the menu."

"To what?"

"Something more *traditional*," she puts on a fake posh accent.

I'm pretty sure Carter's mom thinks this place is beneath her. She's rich as sin and this place is so old school rustic. I imagine she's been turning her nose up at everything. It's difficult to believe someone as sweet and hard working as Carter came from that woman.

"I'll protect you," I tell my cousin.

"God bless you. You remember the sign?" she gives me a side eyed look with a slight tip down of her chin. It makes me laugh.

It's been our *look* since we were kids. The signal we need rescuing from a certain situation.

"Of course I do. I know the assignment."

She breathes out and lets me go. "Thank fuck you're here."

Ashlynn looks beautiful. Her chestnut brown hair is styled in delicate curls that lie on her shoulders. Her make-up is perfect, and she's dressed in a snow-white cable sweater and blue jeans. She's always well turned-out but not pretentious or aloof. She's naturally beautiful and has a heart to match.

For the first time, I see uncertainty in my cousins' eyes. She's overwhelmed, trying not to show it.

"There has got to be something you can do."

The raised voice from around the corner draws her attention. "What's that?"

I quickly explain the situation.

"Surely we can help." Ashlynn worries her lip, drawing it between her teeth.

"He already asked me to switch rooms."

"Is he good looking?"

"That's irrelevant."

Ashlynn peeps around the corner. She turns back slowly. "Holy fuck balls. Girl, never mind switching rooms, invite him to yours."

"This isn't a Hallmark movie."

"It could be though, with a face and body like that."

"He's a stranger."

Ashlynn looks around the corner again. Now her hands are wringing. She's always been a do-gooder and people pleaser. She has to solve everyone's problems, and I see she's already trying to figure out how to help the gorgeous stranger.

"Could you switch rooms just for one night?"

"Ash, come on, don't guilt me into this. You know I need to be in my own room. Besides, who on earth would I share with? My mom? No chance. We're still... not great with each other."

"You're not talking?"

"It's not that. I'm just angry with her."

Ashlynn squeezes my hand.

The door opens and loud voices fill the lobby.

"Speak of the she-devil."

"Don't say that," she scolds me, but there is no real heat behind it. She knows I'm angry at mom for the way she is treating dad. "Your mom has her own room."

"Does Holly?" I query. My sister is with mom. They must have traveled together.

Ashlynn's lips drop open, then quirk up into a grin. Before I can stop her, she is rounding the corner and wading into the chaos that are my mom and sister and three suitcases. Jeez, we're only here for five days.

I should go to my room, avoid talking to mom as long as possible. I'm too curious to see what happens. For a moment, I imagine Holly offering to share rooms with the guy and it makes my stomach turn. Holly got divorced two years ago and ever since she's become a serial dater, devouring men like candy.

The thought of her sharing a room with the handsome stranger almost makes me step out and offer to help. There is a perfectly logical solution to the problem already out there. And one that doesn't involve me sharing a room with someone else.

My curiosity gets the better of me, and I press up to the wall and peer around the corner to watch.

"Nonsense. I'm the one who booked out the place."

"Are you the bride?" I ask, trying to keep the hopeful note out of my voice.

She beams a smile. "I am. And I can't leave you stuck like this. In fact, I think the solution just walked through the door."

We both turn to the two women who are removing all their layers. It reminds me it's cold as shit out there.

"Holly, Aunt Marie, I'm so glad you made it."

Ashlynn walks over and embraces both women. For want of nothing better to do, I take a sip of the hot chocolate.

Damn, that's delicious. I swallow another few mouthfuls, trying not to look as if I'm listening as the bride talks to the two women. She's asking them about sharing their room for a night.

Movement out of the corner of my eye has me looking beyond the reception desk. The sexy blonde from before is staring at me. She's taken off her hat, letting her blond hair fall around her face. Her eyes lock on mine before she ducks away.

It's like that, is it? She can't help out but is too nosey to walk away. I'm distracted from seeing if she is still there by Ashlynn. The two women are tagging along beside her.

"Good news. My aunt and cousin can share tonight, so you can take Holly's room."

"Are you sure? I'm sorry for putting you out like this."

"It's not a problem at all," the younger woman purrs, her eyes taking in every inch of me from my toes to my damp hair.

After formally introducing myself to them, Ashlynn goes to make arrangements for me taking the room tonight. My offer to pay is waved off by all three women. I just got lucky. I'm not complaining. Even as Holly eyes me again.

She looks similar to the other woman peeping around the corner. Not surprising given it's a family wedding. All I want to do now is get my shit out of the truck, thank them profusely, and go to my room.

This is one problem solved. I still need to get to Evergreen Hollow in the morning in time for my meeting. And I need to practice my pitch again. I can't fuck this up.

When everything is sorted, I offer money again but get shot down.

"We've got the whole place. You're going to have to put up with my crazy family. That is payment enough," Ashlynn tells me. "Oh, and we have a get together this evening in the bar. You're welcome to come."

"Thanks, I appreciate that, but I've got a big meeting tomorrow I need to prepare for."

"You should come, Dash. Even if just for a couple of drinks. We're making cocktails," Holly adds, eyeing me like I'm a tasty treat.

If ever there was a reason to stay in my room. Or Holly's room. Crap.

I thank Ashlynn again and politely nod to Holly and Marie, remaining non-committal about attending the party. After getting my overnight bag out of the truck, I head for the stairs. I'm not sure what they're whispering about as I go, and don't really care.

As I round the corner, I expect to see the eavesdropper, but she's gone.

Everywhere is decorated ready for Christmas, including the banisters of the staircase, with garlands and fairy lights.

Upstairs, the rooms are spaced well apart. I find my room number and head inside, setting my overnight bag down on the bed.

The rooms are furnished with reclaimed wooden bed frames, an antique dresser with matching wardrobe. Soft linens in earthy tones give it an old worldly charm. To the left of the door is a bathroom with a claw-foot bathtub and a shower over. There is a white shower curtain pulled back and tied with a Christmas ribbon.

At least it doesn't look like Christmas threw up in here, just a few tasteful decorations and a tray with candles and pinecones on the dresser.

It's not as warm here. It is warm enough to take off the chill, which seeped into my bones while standing outside.

My laptop goes everywhere with me. Thank Christ *that* is still working. I set it on the small desk and sit in the leather chair, powering it up and taking out my phone.

I call my business partner, who is also my sister, and lean back in the chair. Through the window, I see my truck has been moved away from the road, so it's no longer blocking the entrance. More cars are arriving. I should go down and find out what is going to happen to the truck.

First, I need to fill Daria in on the hell I've found myself in.

"I told you to fly," is the first thing she says after I explain my predicament.

"We didn't have enough money for the air fare, Dar, you know that."

"Well, what is it going to cost to get your truck towed, fixed, and road worthy again? Dash, have you seen the weather forecast up there?"

"I've been a little busy to check the weather," I pinch the bridge of my nose. "I'm pretty sure the snow is not about to melt."

"No, that isn't going to happen. They're saying there is going to be at least another five inches of snowfall over the next couple of days."

"Terrific."

"How are you going to get to the meeting?"

"I'll figure something out. I'm not going to let snow stop me from getting to this meeting Dar. It's too important."

"You need to be safe. It'll be no good getting the job if you're not around to do it. Maybe you should fly back, leave that piece of crap truck in a ditch."

"Hey, that truck has got me through a lot."

"A lot of trouble," she chuckles. "Seriously, are you going to be okay? Do I need to do anything to help?"

"No, just stay with the kids and Charlie. Enjoy your time off. Everything will be fine up here."

"You know I can't help worrying about you. You may be my big brother, but you need someone to look after you."

"Thanks for the vote of confidence. I got it handled, sis. I promise. I'll call you as soon as I get out of the meeting."

"Okay," she pauses, and I can picture her twiddling her hair, a nervous habit she's had since she was a toddler. "Dash, we're gonna get the contract, and everything will be great. I can feel it."

"Damn right we are," I agree.

Only I'm not feeling as optimistic as Daria. There is a lot of competition for this contract, from much bigger firms than mine. With even bigger portfolios of work.

Cheering from outside draws my attention. There are a bunch of people all hugging and laughing out front.

As grateful as I am to Ashlynn for giving me this courtesy, I get the feeling things aren't going to be peaceful here tonight. Seeing my truck brings me back to reality with a bump.

"One problem down, one more to go."

A ride to Evergreen Hollow. And the biggest meeting of my life.

The party downstairs is loud.

I've been staring at my proposal for an hour, running through every possible question that might be thrown my way. I pay particular attention to the surrounding area of the proposed plot, to ensure I know everything. I'm sure no one else has considered the rest of the town. Most people are in this for the money.

I mean, we need the money, we need the job, but I won't compromise my morals. I'm a big believer in fitting into the landscape and community. I've learned through working at bigger corporations how badly things can go when you don't consider other people.

Anything I can do to prevent Henrickson Inc being sued, or having people step in to try to stop the build, is one way I'm going to try to swing this.

The noise is distracting. Can't blame these people. They hired out the whole inn so they could party like this.

I shut the laptop. Anything I don't know at this point, I'm never going to know.

My truck is still sitting outside, covered in snow and looking sad and abandoned. So far, I haven't managed to get a rental, but the inn staff promised one of their employees could take me to Evergreen Hollow tomorrow. Weather permitting.

They've been nothing but accommodating and helpful. Everyone I've encountered so far has. When I went downstairs to speak to the staff earlier, a few people passing through the lobby stopped to talk.

I guess one of the four women I met earlier informed them about my predicament. One guy said he's a part-time mechanic and offered to check out the truck, but it wouldn't be until tomorrow.

I'm not holding out any hope it's salvageable at this point. Daria is right, that truck is ready for the scrap heap.

Really, I need a new one, but with money so tight, it hasn't been a priority.

I'm guessing the staff are busy catering to the rest of the guests but I'm hungry. As much as I don't want to intrude, I've got to eat. And I need to get away from these four walls.

Slipping on my boots, I grab my phone and key and head out of the room. Downstairs, the music and chatter are louder.

A couple are sitting in the chairs by the front window. Her legs are thrown over his and he's feeding her something. They seem lost in their own world, oblivious to the other people around them.

"Good evening, Mr. Miller, can I help you?"

"Hi, yeah. I was wondering if the restaurant is open, or maybe I can get some food sent up to my room given how busy it is."

"Of course, that won't be a problem. I apologize if you called down?"

"No, that's fine, I didn't call. I wanted to check it out first. And..." Looking at the group of people and hearing the raucous laughter, I let her know with a look I prefer to go back to the room. She nods knowingly.

"Dash!"

Ashlynn comes through the archway from the bar, a huge smile on her face. She looks stunning in a long flowing red dress with crystals around the top half which glitter in the soft light of the lobby.

A tall, fair-haired man, who looks like he could bench press a car, has one hand on her hip. He's wearing a dark shirt and dress pants, with a red tie, and is holding a cocktail in the other hand.

"You should come join us," Ashlynn says.

Before I can protest, she is pulling the giant man around to face me.

"Carter, this is Dash, the guy I told you about with the broken-down truck."

"Nice to meet you," he reaches out a giant hand and I give it a quick shake. "Sorry about your truck. Leon said he can look at it in the morning. He's an amazing mechanic. If anyone can fix a vehicle, it's Leon."

"Yeah, I spoke to him earlier."

"Bad luck having that happen up here. Especially with the forecast."

"I heard about that."

"Five more inches. It's perfect," Ashlynn leans into Carter.

"You're nuts babe," he kisses her cheek. "It's already crazy heavy out there, we don't need more snow," he looks back to me. "She's obsessed with all things Christmas."

My smile is polite. They're nice enough people but I'm starving and not in the mood to socialize.

"Did I hear you asking about the restaurant?" Ashlynn turns her attention back on me. "You seriously haven't eaten? Come on, we have a ton of food."

Ashlynn spins and heads for the bar which I'm presuming leads on to the dining room.

"You don't have to. I can tell her you got food up in your room," Carter tells me. "Don't feel bad about it. She'll have already bumped into someone else to talk to."

"I can't intrude. You guys have already done enough for me, and this is a family thing."

"The offer is there, but if you want to duck out, I'll let Ash know."

My first thought is to thank him so I can make a quick one eighty and go back upstairs. Until another red dress catches my eye. I stop dead, all thoughts leaving my brain.

Fuck, I thought she was hot all wrapped up in a huge coat and hat, but damn.

Her dress is similar to Ashlynn's. It's tight all the way down where Ashlynn's flares out. It has the same tiny crystals that glimmer as every light hits it. Her hair is swept up in a messy but organized style. She has that insanely hot red lipstick on again.

It's only Carter's low laugh that has my attention snapping back to the reality of where I'm standing.

"I think it's best if I go back upstairs."

Carter laughs, understanding my meaning. Good job he doesn't take offence at it. I'm not sure what his relationship is to the woman. He pats my shoulder and heads after his wife-to-be.

It's time to make my escape.

"Dash!"

Fuck.

Holly and Marie approach. Marie looks three sheets to the wind, carrying a cocktail. Holly's smiling broadly at me. She's wearing a black cocktail dress with a red flower pattern that hugs her figure, and she's straightened her short blonde hair. She looks good but not as good as the woman in the red dress.

"I'm so glad you made it," Holly touches my arm. "Come inside, you have got to try the signature cocktail they've been teaching us. It's to die for."

Marie is nodding along. She shows me her glass to reiterate the fact. My protest is lost as the two women railroad me through the door to the bar. Jesus Christ. The only way to get out of this would make me come off a complete asshole.

I admit defeat.

Everyone is dressed up and jovial, clearly enjoying the party. The inn's restaurant and bar are all in one large space, with the dining tables to the rear. During the day it would be homely and cozy but it's decorated for the party. And Christmas. It's tasteful with red accents everywhere, including on the guests. I guess it's a theme.

I'm so out of place, it's kind of embarrassing.

A counter is set up by the bar with the detritus of the cocktail lesson I've heard about. Two men in all black are chatting by the counter but one comes over when Holly asks for a cocktail for me.

I try to tell her I only want a beer because I have a big day, but she shushes me. Best to just go with it. They both wait patiently, staring expectantly as I taste it. It's nice, a little sweet for my taste but I smile and nod making them happy.

They chat about the wedding and the plans for the next few days. I happily inform them I won't be around. I'll be leaving tomorrow after my meeting and the truck being sorted.

Holly keeps touching my arm when she asks questions. And flicking her hair. I'm not blind, or an idiot, I'm just not interested.

"So, Dash, where are you from? I feel like we've been doing all the talking," Holly says.

Looks like I'm not getting away with this. "Cheyenne."

"Is that near here?"

One look at Marie says she doesn't know her geography. "It's about a three-hour drive from here."

"It's in Wyoming?" Holly asks.

"Yeah, to the south of here. It's the capital."

Holly laughs and touches her neck. I'm not the kind of guy who judges people by their knowledge. What I do get pissed about, is when people ask me questions they don't care to know the answers to.

"Oh, we're from South Carolina," Holly tells me.

"You've traveled a long way."

"Ashlynn is so obsessed with Christmas and winter and snow," Holly rolls her eyes.

"Maybe it's about more than just winter and snow," I suggest. "Wyoming is a beautiful state."

"Of course it is," Holly laughs and touches my shirt just over my pec.

I raise my cocktail to surreptitiously shift her arm away, and take a long sip. Over my glass, I spot the woman in the red dress. She's framed by one of the large windows overlooking the back patio. The fairy lights highlight her, and I find myself staring.

Everything around me disappears as my eyes travel over her. She's absolutely gorgeous.

She laughs at something the man standing with her says. An irrational need to go over and find out what the hell he is saying, and who he is to her, takes over. Logic says he's a relative, but that isn't necessarily true.

As she turns her head, our eyes lock. I swear she pauses, does a double take and her lips part slightly. But the moment is over as fast as it began, and she returns to her conversation.

It takes a moment for me to realize Holly is trying to get my attention.

"Sorry?" I look back at her.

She glances across to where I was looking and her eyes narrow.

"I wouldn't bother," she says with a huff.

"Bother?"

"With her. She hates men."

That might explain why she didn't want to give up her room to one. Getting into a conversation about a woman I'm insanely attracted to, with one who is clearly showing jealousy, is my idea of trouble.

It's time I extricate myself from this. My stomach is growling so loud it's going to be heard over the music and chatter. Before I can make my excuses Marie speaks up.

"Holly, don't talk about your sister like that."

Now it's my turn to do a double take. There is a resemblance but everything about the other woman is turned up to a ten. I feel like a prick for thinking it. But as is often the case, my mouth opens before my brain engages.

"She is *your* sister?"

And from the look on Holly's face, that is definitely the wrong thing to say.

Chapter 3

THE NIGHT HAS BEEN amazing. Seeing Ashlynn so happy is a dream come true for me. She went through so much with her ex. He was a raging pile of dog shit who dared lay his hands on her. I only wish she'd told me sooner. Unfortunately for that asshole, when she did tell me, I convinced her to tell her brothers, and they dealt with the bastard.

Finding Carter, someone sweet and caring and manly and heroic, and all the other words I could use to describe him, is the best thing to ever happen to her.

She deserves the world, and Carter is more than happy to give it to her.

We spent the afternoon running through the plans for the coming days, drinking and catching up with family and friends we haven't seen in a while.

It's a testament to how much Ashlynn and Carter are loved that everyone flew out here for the wedding. It's not your typical destination wedding either, given the weather. But everyone is more than happy to be here.

The inn is gorgeous. It's everything I imagine a small-town, rustic and romantic inn would be. It's not entirely my speed but something I could happily spend this week enjoying.

Ashlynn has swept me up in her love of snow too. Despite how damn cold it is, I enjoyed the brief walk she took me on through the fields at the back of the inn. Until I could no longer feel my toes that is. The raging fire in the lobby was a welcome relief after that walk.

The cocktail making lesson was a stroke of genius on my cousin's part. I've never seen my family have so much fun. For the most part we were sensible but one of my uncles got carried away thinking he was in the movie 'Cocktail,' and ended up shattering a bottle of gin trying to throw it.

After that, we were put into two groups to come up with a signature cocktail, one for the bride and one for the groom. I ended up on Team Carter. We came up with a spin on a mojito, using all the usual ingredients but adding coconut milk to make it white, like snow.

I would have preferred we came up with a better name, but Carter christened it *Ashlynn's Kiss.* He got a lot of stick for it, but he didn't care.

Our rivals came up with *Born to Rum Punch* which Ashlynn found hilarious.

She wasn't laughing when the cocktail instructors tasted the cocktails to give their final verdict, and we won by a country mile. Someone was way too liberal with the *splash* of rum they were supposed to use in Ashlynn's cocktail. She didn't mind, she was too enamored with the name of Carter's.

The night is going perfectly. What I didn't expect to see, was the guy whose truck broke down.

He looks so out of place it's almost comical. The theme for tonight is black and red and, for the most part, people have followed the brief. This guy is in blue jeans and a checked shirt over a white T.

I wouldn't put it past Ashlynn to have invited him. She wouldn't shut up about him this afternoon, telling me I was stupid not to offer him my room. With me in it.

She told me his name is Dash, making a joke about all the Christmas names. As in mine and my sisters. I wasn't sure where she was going with Dash being a Christmas name. She said it was for Dasher, the reindeer.

I highly doubt his name is Dasher. We laughed about it as Ashlynn painted her toenails, dreaming up ways for me to find out what his real name is.

Not going to happen. The guy is here for one night. He's stranded, stuck with us. I bet he can't wait for morning to get the hell out of here.

For the past twenty minutes, I've watched in silent amusement as he fended off my sister's advances. He's done a decent job. The hair flicking, throat touching and trailing her fingers over his chest don't appear to faze him. He must get hit on all the time.

It's probably killing Holly not getting anything back.

So far, I've managed to avoid catching his eye, instead having the opportunity to stare at him at my leisure. He really is good looking, his shirt sleeves are rolled up showing off his tanned forearms.

His presence here hasn't gone unnoticed by the women in the room. I've heard more than one person asking who he is. Everyone assumes he's one of Carter's friends. He looks as if he would fit in with the firefighters.

There is a quiet intensity in his eyes as he observes everything around him. Who can blame him being thrust into this crazy family gathering? With Holly to top it all off.

I do feel bad for not offering up my room. The only options available to me where to share with mom or Holly, neither of which appealed.

One of Ashlynn's brothers is cracking jokes next to me and I laugh at a particularly childish one, just as my eyes lock on *him*.

Jesus, he's staring right at me. Crap, I can't let him see me staring back. Oh God, I turn away, my cheeks flushing. Totally smooth. How do I get out of his line of sight without it looking obvious?

I risk a sneaky look back and see my sister glaring at me. She says something to him, his head swings back to her, and he responds. Whatever he says, Holly does not look happy. In fact, she looks back at me even more irritated than before.

I don't have time for Holly's theatrics. I excuse myself from the group and head back into the dining area to get away from their stares.

A tray of hot spring rolls has just been replaced so I grab one and nibble on it, walking to the patio doors to look at the deck out back. There is a large patio with two fire pits, and string lights illuminating the space. It's surrounded by shrubs and potted plants. They're all hanging heavy with snow.

My eyes widen. Wow, there is a whole hell of a lot more snow out there now than there was earlier. I've heard people talking about the forecast but seeing it is a shock.

"I can't believe how much has come down in the last couple of hours."

I almost jump out of my skin at the voice behind me. It's Dash. He's holding a plate of food and is staring through the window with a frown.

"It's a lot," I agree. I go to brush some hair behind my ear and realize, almost too late, I'm still holding the spring roll. His lip tilts up in a half smirk. "You managed to get a room," I say to take the focus off me almost putting food in my hair.

"Yeah, your sister's. She gave hers up for me."

Sounds right. I keep that thought to myself. From the way he's looking at me, he knows exactly what I'm thinking. He got the measure of my sister in their very short interaction.

"The options open to me would have been sharing with her or my mom and," I glance over at them. Mom has gone and Holly is with a couple of our other bitchier cousins. No doubt talking about me. "And no offence," I turn back to Dash. "You're a stranger, and my sanity and privacy were more important."

"A half hour ago I would have said offence is very much taken. Kidding," he shakes his head with a wry laugh. "I'm the one who got myself into this mess. I'm just glad there was a way around it. I don't blame you for not wanting to give up your room."

He's right. I'm not going to apologize for it. We stare at each other in silence for a few moments. I'm not a shy person by nature and I've never had a problem talking to men. This guy has me tongue-tied.

"Well I-"

"What are you-"

We speak at the same time. Then both say, 'you go first' and then we laugh.

"Go on," he says.

"I was just going to say what are you going to do about your truck? You weren't planning on stopping here, obviously."

"No, I have a meeting in the next town over. Getting there might be a problem. The hotel has offered me a ride," he looks out of the window again. "But this storm is getting worse."

"Driving probably wouldn't be the best idea."

"That's gonna be a pain in the ass for me."

"Is it an important meeting?"

"The biggest of my life," he sighs. "Do you mind if we sit, I'm starving, and this is going cold."

Oh. He's inviting me to join him? It's not the worst idea in the world. There are plenty of people here to chat with, but I'm intrigued by Dash.

The biggest meeting of his life?

I'm kind of nosey and own that. I'm happy to join him if I can find out what is going on.

We head to a table and sit opposite each other. Ashlynn is staring at me. One hand rushes to cover her mouth as she tries to hide the excitement. I'm going to hear about this tomorrow.

"I don't mean to sound rude here, but what is your name?"

"You mean my sister didn't tell you?"

"No," he takes a bite of burger slider.

"What did she say?"

"Nothing important."

"Let me guess, I'm a man hater?"

He doesn't answer, which tells me two things about this. One, that is what Holly said. And two, he's a good guy who doesn't repeat shit he knows is rude. I'm not upset. Not in the slightest. In fact, its old news.

The thing with my immediate family is, Holly has always been jealous of me. It started practically from birth because I got more attention than her. She was almost four when I was born so it was more noticeable to her when the baby was being fawned over. It continued as we grew older.

The rivalry is stupid. I try not to play up to it but when she started flirting with my boyfriends, it was a step too far. When I left for college, I didn't keep in touch with her, only hearing about what was going on in her life through our parents. I'm not sure where she got the idea I hate men, probably from abruptly dumping two of my boyfriends, because they chose to reciprocate her flirting.

Mom is a different story. We have always been fine in the past. I can turn to her in my time of need, but I've always been closer with my dad. The divorce has divided us. Mom's behavior towards dad is really upsetting.

Having him barred from this event was the final straw for me.

Sharing a room with either of them was always out of the question, even if I do feel bad about turning Dash down.

"Eve," I tell him, in answer to his initial question.

"Holly and Eve?" he glances around the room. "Your family has a real thing for Christmas."

"We're not all as obsessed as Ashlynn," I laugh, popping the rest of the spring roll into my mouth.

"I'm Dash," he reaches his hand across to me and we shake. "I gotta say, when I left home this morning, this is not where I expected to end up."

"You live around here?"

"Cheyenne, south of here."

"Wyoming's state capital." He looks up, impressed. "I had an interest in geography when I was a kid. Where most kids had pictures of pop stars or actors on the wall, I had a map of the US and a huge world map. I used to put pins in the places I wanted to go."

"Was Wyoming one of them?" he grins.

"Sorry, no. I never thought I'd end up here either."

We stare some more. I clear my throat.

"So, what is this big meeting?"

He lets out a heavy sigh and his expression becomes more pensive. I feel bad about asking. It looks like I've brought the mood down.

"I'm putting in a bid to build a hotel complex up in Evergreen Hollow."

"You're in construction?"

"Yeah. Getting this contract would set up my company for the next couple of years."

"That is a big deal. If you can't make it, will they give you another shot?"

"That's the question," he leans back in his chair and turns to look out of the window again.

I follow his gaze, the snow is really coming down. Ashlynn has a back-up plan for the ceremony. She did want to hold it outside, but it's looking more and more like that isn't a possibility.

The patio can be closed in though and the hotel has pictures of other events they've held there. There is also an indoor event room.

"Won't they give you some grace, considering the storm?"

"It's a highly sought after contract. I'm not the only one bidding. My company is small in comparison to the others. If they can all get there, I have to too."

"It means something that you've got a chance to meet them. They must like what they see."

"I thought so. The problem is, they're already running behind and it's costing them money," he can see I'm not sure what that means. "It's all boring information about the land and zoning and other things. Point is, I don't think they'll give me a second chance."

"You need to get there, no matter what?"

"Yep."

"Fingers crossed it slows down overnight," I say, sympathetically.

He gives me a wry smile.

"Eve, we're taking pictures." One of my aunts appears in the dining room, which I realize is empty besides me and Dash. "Carter said to come get you."

"Be right there," I call back. Dash gives me another devastating smile. God, he makes my insides sizzle. It's been a while since that happened. Ten months to be exact. This is the longest dry spell I've had. "I better go. I hope things work out."

"I'm sure they will."

He winks and my heart swoops into my stomach. Leaving him to his meal, I head back to the bar to join in the chaos of the self-appointed photographer, Ashlynn's dad. He's trying to wrangle everyone out into the lobby to take shots with the fireplace and Christmas tree.

As we're all being moved about by height size, I watch Dash slip past and head to the stairs, going up to his, Holly's, room. Out of the corner of my eye, I notice my sister watching him too and scowl.

"Eve! Smile," my uncle calls. "This is a happy occasion."

Everyone laughs and I roll my eyes. Even as I smile, my thoughts are on Dash. He didn't go into detail, but I get the feeling this contract is more than a big deal for his company.

It sounded like a deal breaker.

As soon as I wake up, I hop out of bed and pull back the curtains. I stopped drinking after the photos last night, even if I stayed up late. Getting Dash's predicament out of my head was near on impossible.

It isn't snowing but what is on the ground is deep. As I watch, inn staff come out to shovel the paths and lay down grit.

The SUV I rented has snow tires and was pretty good at getting me here. It has a high safety rating.

I can't believe I'm even considering this but something about his demeanor last night told me Dash really needs to get to this meeting.

Evergreen Hollow is only about forty miles away. It would take less than an hour to drive there. Leaning against the wall, watching the men shoveling the snow, I bite my lip. Is this a good idea or not? Do I offer to take him?

The hotel did say they could arrange it. I mean, it's not my place to step in. He has it handled.

My stomach growls. I didn't get much food last night. After taking a quick shower and dressing in jeans and a black V-neck knit sweater, I slip on my boots, grab my keys and head downstairs.

I'm going to get food. It's no big deal if I take a detour to reception and ask about how bad it will be to drive on the roads. And it doesn't matter so much if I question whether they're able to provide another guest with a ride, because I have a decent vehicle that could make the journey.

It is a different woman on the desk from when I checked in yesterday, so she doesn't know about me refusing to give Dash my room. She does know about his request for a ride.

"We can take him there, but our staff can't hang around waiting to bring him back, which I know isn't terribly helpful but as you know, we're very busy here. We could arrange for a cab to bring him back."

"Okay, thanks..." I bite my nail.

"Eve Dalton. A word if I may."

Crap. I turn to Ashlynn. Even though she had her fair share of cocktails last night, my cousin doesn't look any worse for wear. In fact, she looks gorgeous in a camel-colored dress with brown panty hose and knee-high black boots.

She approaches the desk and smiles at the receptionist.

"Could you please tell Dash Miller when he comes down that I'd like a word before he heads out."

"Of course."

"Thank you so much. We'll be in the dining room."

Ashlynn links her arm in mine and drags me away from the desk. She finds a table out of the way, smiling and waving at some of the people already here. Not a word passes her lips until we're sitting opposite one another. Even then, she stares at me.

"What?"

A smile spreads across her gloss painted lips.

"Shut up."

"Didn't say anything." She smiles at the server who offers us coffee, turning over our cups so she can fill them up.

I add two sugars and some cream while Ashlynn watches me with that stupid look on her face.

"Okay, so maybe I feel bad for him."

"Hm mm," she stirs sugar into her own coffee.

"He has an important meeting in another town and his truck is..."

"Buried in a foot of snow and not going anywhere any time soon?"

"Yeah, that," I mutter.

"It's very sweet of you to offer to take him."

"I haven't."

Her eyes narrow. "I have a really good feeling about him, you know."

"You and your feelings," I drink some coffee. It scalds my tongue, and I wince.

"I've never been wrong before."

"You're wrong about this." I pick up the menu and peruse the options, laughing at the Christmas themed names.

North pole breakfast bowl for oatmeal with caramelized apples, toasted pecans and maple syrup. Or eggnog French toast and Holiday scramble. The cinnamon spiced pancakes sound really good.

"You forget I know you. Holly wasn't the only one making googly eyes at him last night."

Over the years, I've learned arguing with her when she is in a mood like this, gets me nowhere. Instead, I wave over the server and order the delicious sounding pancakes.

"I'll have the winter berry parfait," Ashlynn smiles sweetly. "Got to fit into that dress in four days."

"You look great."

"Flattery will not distract me."

"Look, I feel bad not helping him out the first time around. It's no big deal. I have a really good car, like stupidly good for driving in the snow."

"Oh, I'm *all* for it," she grins maniacally. "What time is his meeting?"

"I'm not his secretary."

"You were very cozy last night," she whispers.

"We were like this," I move my hand in a gesture between the two of us. "Across a table. I didn't ask for details. I wasn't planning to offer him a ride until this morning."

"Morning Dash," Ashlynn exclaims, much louder than the question she asked me. She is grinning at someone over my shoulder.

My mouth drops open, and I glare at her, mouthing, 'you bitch'. She *knew* he was standing there.

"Morning," Dash moves so he is standing between us at the side of the table.

It takes a good seven seconds for me to raise my eyes. He gives me an odd look before he turns to Ashlynn. My eyes can't help the once over. He's wearing suit pants and a shirt. He's prepared for his meeting.

"They said at reception you wanted to talk to me?"

"Yes, please sit. Do you want some coffee?"

Looking amused, Dash takes a seat to the left of Ashlynn, facing me. He welcomes the coffee but declines any food.

"As I'm sure you just heard, my amazing friend here thought you might need a ride this morning and given she has nothing to do, she's hoping you take her up on the offer."

Her look tells me not to contradict her.

Nothing to do? We have a whole schedule of plans for today. And like reception said, they can't leave their staff member hanging around. They have no idea how long he will be there. It was just an idea to take him, I wasn't really thinking about doing it...

That's a lie.

"I can't let you do that. There is a lot of snow out there."

"What about how important the meeting is?" I ask, going against my conflicted thoughts.

"I'm gonna see if they'll let me conference call."

"From what you said last night they might not appreciate a compromise like that."

Ashlynn is smirking wide now. Our food arrives, pausing the conversation.

"We all know this is really important, and one of us would take you without question if we didn't have so much to do," Ashlynn tells Dash as she toys with some fruit on her dish. "This is the perfect plan."

Dash keeps his gaze on me. He doesn't believe Ashlynn. As well he shouldn't. He's waiting for *me* to agree. I would be grateful if someone offered me this chance if I were in their shoes.

"Yeah, she's right. I'd be happy to."

Chapter 4

I OFFER TO TAKE her car, so she doesn't have to come along. I don't let on being alone in a car with her will be a pleasant distraction from what I am facing today.

An issue with the rental insurance means I can't drive it. It would cost a lot to upgrade, given the conditions on the road. Ashlynn is very much against the idea of us trying to sort the insurance out.

In my room, I quickly call Daria to let her know I've got a ride to Evergreen Hollow.

"Thank God, Dash. I was worried. We got another bill through," she adds quietly.

I hate hearing the defeated tone in her voice. I'm not sure what we are going to do if we don't get this contract. Sure, we can try to find smaller jobs that will bring in money.

It won't be enough to cover half of our costs.

"It's going to be okay, Daria."

She takes a deep breath, pulling herself together. Daria has always been the positive one out of the two of us and hearing the doubt in her voice worries me.

"You're right. You can do this," she says. "Your pitch is brilliant. Our plans are perfect. They'd be stupid not to choose us for the job."

"Keep thinking those thoughts, sis."

"I have every faith in you. Did you have any luck with your truck?" Daria asks.

"One of the guys here is a mechanic. Once they dig the fucking thing out of the snow, he's going to take a look. I'll worry about that when I get back. I'll call you as soon as I'm done."

"You better. Good luck."

When we hang up, I stare around the room. Once the pitch is over, it could take a few days for them to decide, likely after the holidays given how close it is to Christmas. I'll worry about getting back to Cheyenne once this is over.

For the millionth time I make sure the laptop is charged and I've packed the charger, just in case. I pocket my phone, straighten my tie and stare at myself in the mirror. I'm not a suit wearing kind of guy and feel uncomfortable in it. Impressing these people is priority number one. I need this job.

"Don't fuck it up," I tell my reflection. "Good pep talk," it replies.

Fuck, I'm losing my mind.

Downstairs, I round the corner to the lobby and almost bump right into Holly.

"Dash, I was just going to see if I could find you."

"Uh," I glance around but don't see Eve.

"Would you like to join me for breakfast?" she asks.

"Thank you for the offer, but I'm heading out."

"You're leaving?" she practically gasps.

"I have a meeting in another town."

"Will you be back later?"

"Yeah, only long enough to get my things. You can have your room back as promised."

She touches her collar bone, sliding her shirt out of the way to reveal some cleavage. I studiously avoid lowering my eyes.

"Promise we can at least get a drink before you go."

Jeez this woman doesn't give up. Eve comes around the corner and sees me talking to her sister. I go to call her over, but she shakes her head. Before Holly can turn around, I tell her it depends on what time I get back, but I'll let her know. Eve slips out of the door without alerting her sister.

There has gotta be a story there. I take my leave of Holly and head outside.

"Damn," I shiver, pulling my coat around me.

Standing on the porch I look at the area surrounding the inn. In my home state, I'm more than used to the freezing cold winters. I've always loved the beauty of it.

Maybe it's because I'm used to dirty snow and people complaining about the storms that I'm awe struck. The snow up here is pristine, with a slight sparkle where the sun reflects off it. The trees around here are evergreens with snow hanging from the leafy boughs. The sky is so blue it's almost blinding.

And then there is Eve, standing beside a large white SUV with dark rear windows and, thankfully, snow tires. She's pulled that fluffy pink hat on over her blonde hair and is wearing a hip-length jacket that is belted at the middle. Her long legs are clad in skintight jeans tucked into gray boots.

A scarf that matches the hat is wrapped twice around her neck, it's so long. She won't need that once we're on the road in the heated car, but it is cold as balls outside.

All thoughts of Holly and her cleavage leave my head. Not that I'd cared one way or another about her cleavage. Damn, Eve isn't showing even an inch of skin, beside her face, and I'm feeling a stirring in the pit of my stomach.

She waves me over and climbs in the driver seat. Shaking out of the lust induced stupor, I head down the stairs, almost slipping in the stupid fucking shoes.

Before I get inside, I notice Holly on the porch, watching me get into Eve's car. That woman seems to be everywhere. And again, she doesn't look happy.

"What's the deal with you and your sister?" I ask as I slam the door shut.

Eve looks back to the inn, then starts the car.

"You snuck out of there like you didn't want her to see you," I add.

"We don't have time for questions, and she'd ask a million. In case you haven't noticed," she turns her head to face me. "She's got a thing for you."

There is no point arguing. She's right. Eve smirks.

We set out and once we're on the road away from the inn, I give her directions. For a while, we travel in silence. I don't want to break her concentration while we're on roads that haven't been plowed properly.

My pitch is swarming around my head. I can do this. I can win this contract. Building this hotel is the only thing I want. I'll do anything to get it. To take the fear out of my sister's voice. And the worry it's causing her. Her husband has a job, but Daria is the breadwinner in their house, losing her salary would affect them in a bad way.

Having that responsibility on my shoulders should spur me on, not make me nervous.

"Do you have a presentation to give or are you just talking to these guys?" Eve's voice breaks through my thoughts.

"A presentation and pitch. I don't doubt my presentation. I don't doubt my plans for the building."

"But you doubt yourself?" she asks after a moment of silence.

"There is a lot riding on it. A lot of people will be let down if I fail."

"Well, if you're gonna think like that, you're setting yourself up to fail. You just said you don't doubt your ability and your design. Don't get in your own way."

"Are you going to tell me to picture everyone naked?"

"Depends on what they look like," she grins.

"Two guys in their mid-sixties. There is a younger guy, around my age. He'd intimidate me if I saw him naked."

Eve laughs, and it takes the edge off my nerves a little.

"How about we change the subject?" she suggests, understanding I'm not handling this well.

She tells me about the wedding plans and how long Ashlynn has been dreaming of a 'white' wedding.

It's a welcome break from the never-ending cycle of construction plans running through my head. Not to mention environmentally friendly design and materials. Timelines, workforce and unforeseen challenges.

Shit, I've got a truck load of those.

It helps to take my mind off everything for a while the more I listen to her voice. She switches to her own life back in South Carolina. She is in public relations and marketing and works in the food industry.

On the home straight into Evergreen Hollow, we pass by a large billboard sign.

"Could you slow down a second? Actually, can you pull over?"

Eve looks concerned but does as I ask. The roads have been clear and the skies mercifully free of snow. Traffic has been sparse, so she has no bother pulling to the side of the road. I get out of the car once Eve turns off the engine, and walk to the edge of the field.

Her car door opens and closes, and she comes to stand beside me. Using both hands to shield her eyes, she looks across the massive expanse of land.

"This is it," I tell her.

"What?"

"Where the hotel is going to be."

"Here," she looks across the field. There isn't much around. "There is nothing here."

"The plan is to expand. The mayor wants to make the town bigger, more appealing to tourists. There is a lot of natural beauty around this area. Tourists come for the national parks but have to stay out of town. He wants them to bring their business here."

"And their plan is to build a hotel in the middle of all this natural beauty?" Eve drops her hands and looks at me accusingly.

I get it. This is my home state, I don't want the rural, natural areas to end up like a big city. "My aim is to blend it into the area, not destroy it."

"I wish you'd shown me the plans before we left," she turns back to the land. "I can't picture it."

We're running ahead of schedule so I suggest if we have enough time, we can grab a coffee nearby where the meeting is. I'll happily show her my plans.

Despite my nerves, I'm proud of this building. Daria is an amazing architect. Between that and my engineering degree, we've come up with an amazing building.

Eve steers us into a parking lot. There's no coffee shop nearby but there is one in the lobby of the office, so we head inside.

"I should have asked if you wanted to practice your pitch," Eve says, hurrying alongside me.

"If I don't know it by now, there is no point me going in there."

"You'll be fine," she says with such conviction, I almost believe her.

We grab a seat in a quiet corner. I set up the laptop while she goes to get us coffee. This is another situation I didn't think I would find myself in. If anything, I thought she'd drop me off then go do her own thing.

When Eve comes back, she sits close. Her intoxicating scent surrounds me. I'm not sure what it is, but it's amazing. She sets my cup by me, and I fidget, pulling at my tie. I feel like it's choking me.

"Why are you wearing a tie if it's making you uncomfortable?"

"Because I have to make a good impression."

"I hate to break it to you, Dash. You've been tugging on that tie and pulling a face every time you do. It's the furthest thing from a good impression. You don't usually wear ties, huh?"

"That obvious."

"Yeah, actually," she laughs and sips from her cup. "Okay, show me the building, then we'll work on you."

"What does that mean?"

"Trust me."

I'm not sure I like the sound of that. She leans close when I open the design program on my laptop. I never use blueprints. My company is one hundred percent paperless. Eve listens attentively as I explain about the energy efficient design, sustainable materials, and the intuitive technology that will power the building. Everything is eco-friendly, right down to the fabrics for the bedrooms.

She asks a lot of questions about the plans for the hotel to be set into the terrain. It will be aesthetically pleasing for the area as well as the people who live in Evergreen Hollow. I don't want it to have a detrimental effect on the town at all.

"You should lead with that," she says.

"With what?"

"How passionate you are about the area, the people who live here."

"I'm not sure that is what they want to hear, but I will raise it. It's a big part of what my company stands for."

"Why do you think they don't want to hear it?"

"They're a huge corporation, they don't care about the little people."

The thought annoys me. It goes against everything I believe in.

"Dash, I might not have known you long, but having talked with you and seen a couple of different sides of you, I can tell which one people prefer."

"Two different sides?" What does that even mean?

"This is not the real you, the guy in the suit, conforming to what you think other people want. That might be the way your competitors handle stuff, but it doesn't sit right with you."

"I need this contract."

Her lips twist as she looks back at the design. "It's just, that," she points at the screen, then turns her finger on me. "And this, don't go together."

I run a hand through my hair and stare at the screen. She's right. But there are way too many people depending on me landing this contract. I can't afford to be *the real me*.

"What's the name of the company you're meeting?"

I'm about to ask why but give her the details. She pulls my laptop around and opens a browser window. Not sure what she is doing, I drink my coffee, watching her lips move as she reads from the site. Is it hot in here? I tug at my collar again, drawing her attention for a moment. Eve frowns then focuses on the laptop.

My palms are starting to sweat and my stomach clenches. It's almost time for me to go upstairs and let them know I'm here.

"Okay, this guy," she spins the laptop to me showing me the bio of one of the company directors. It's the younger guy. He's the son of one of the older men and is on a fast track to take over. I know at least that much.

"What about him?"

"First off, I think you're right. He'd really intimidate you if he got naked," she smirks. "Joking aside, read this, his statement about buildings of the future."

Leaning close I read through the bio. A lot of what he is saying is like my ethos about the future of construction. Why didn't I know this?

"That is who you need to pitch to."

"I can't ignore the two major shareholders in their firm."

"No, but I think you can win him over. If you win him over, you'll be steps ahead of the competition. This guy will be running the company soon. One of the others is getting ready to retire, it says so right on their website. And look at this," she flips to another page and shows me articles about sustainable and energy efficient buildings, and how important they are for the future of the planet.

"If you want my advice, and I know you don't need to take it, you know your industry better than me. I think you need to lose the tie, unbutton the collar and talk about what this building can do for Evergreen Hollow. How it will attract big names, how it will benefit the community and last long into the future."

"Look, I appreciate the advice, I do. But this... It's too important."

Eve nods.

We both glance up as the elevator opens and three men come out. They're dressed in suits and are holding blueprints and briefcases. They are all stony faced.

"Do you think they're here for the contract too?"

"Yeah, that's Devon Bright Industries."

They're all a bunch of assholes. They've won way too many contracts over me. One of them spots me as they're approaching the door and does a double take. Fucking ass. He smirks and straightens his jacket then follows the other two outside.

"Friend of yours?" Eve asks. I arch a brow in response. "They didn't look overly confident. There was no joy in their faces. They probably talked about rebars and steel reinforcements and, you know, concrete."

A laugh bursts out of me. She's right about one thing, they all looked fucking miserable. Could she be right about the rest of it? It's a huge risk. To go against everything I've been telling myself for weeks.

The environment is my passion. When I was talking to Eve about the plans, it didn't enter my head to be nervous. I got lost in the idea of it all.

"You should go up," Eve says. "Whatever you decide to do, you'll be great."

I gather up all my stuff and pull my collar again.

"Dash," Eve steps up close. "Do whatever is best but please, take this off," she reaches for my tie.

My body freezes as I watch her loosen and pull the knot out. The second it's untied, I feel like I can breathe again.

Except now I'm staring at Eve as she slowly pulls the tie out from beneath my collar.

My mind conjures up a very different scenario. For a moment I picture her using the tie to tug me closer to her, so she can press her lips against mine.

Is it wrong to ask for a good luck kiss?

I clear my throat, and her eyes lift to mine. Up close I notice the darker colored ring around her blue irises. She steps back and takes the tie with her, holding it hostage. I'm not about to argue. I don't want it back.

"That's better," she says quietly. "This looks more like the man I'm starting to see you are."

"Thanks," I croak out, clearing my throat again.

Eve grabs my laptop and hands it to me, then folds up my tie and puts it in her pocket. "You can burn this when you get the contract," she grins.

I laugh and nod. Neither of us says another word. It's odd, I feel a renewed sense of myself. Of who I am. The suit wearing, knee bending, pandering to what I think other people want me to be, isn't who I am.

As the elevator glides up to the fifth floor, I stare at my reflection in the mirrored door. Am I really going to completely change the pitch I've been practicing for weeks? Put my entire livelihood in jeopardy?

For months I've convinced myself I don't stand a chance of winning this contract. I've put on a brave face for everyone around me. Maybe, if I do take a chance, I might pull this off.

The doors open and I walk over to the smiling receptionist.

With every step my determination comes back. My spine straightens a little more, and my heart feels less like it's about to combust in my chest.

"Hi, Dash Miller, I'm here to meet with Henrickson Inc."

Chapter 5

I'VE NEVER BEEN SO tense in my life over something I have absolutely nothing invested in. Here I am thinking I'm just giving Dash a ride to his meeting. Then he made me stop at the site where they're planning to build this hotel. And I got really annoyed.

I didn't let on to Dash, because arguing with him would be unfair. My rage was tightly sealed up.

Until he showed me his plans. Everything about them is mind-blowing. He thought of everything that could be used to make the building completely eco-friendly. Right down to the organic cotton materials to furnish the hotel rooms with. The water conservation plans are out of this world.

Now, I'm rooting for him with everything I have. I'm not a religious person at all, so praying is pointless, but I do make a small plea into the universe for him. It would do this town a disservice to get a bawdy, concrete and glass monstrosity built here.

I looked up Devon Bright Industries as soon as Dash disappeared into the elevator. All their buildings are the same. There is a small effort put into elements of environmental awareness in their buildings. Nothing like Dash's. His is entirely focused on it.

I check his website as I sip on another coffee. There is a picture of him on the home page. I can't help but think this is how he should have presented himself today. In a t-shirt and open shirt, smiling at the camera. It's a professional photo. He looks carefree and casual, like someone you would want to build a multi-million-dollar hotel for you.

His business partner is a pretty brunette, who I know from the 'about' page, is his sister. She is an architect and has a lot to do with the design of the building, while Dash is the engineering and construction side. It seems like a great company. The buildings in their gallery are all beautiful.

There is nothing as grand as a whole ass hotel. This really is a big deal for them.

If these jerks don't choose him for this contract, they'll be making a huge mistake.

My phone buzzes in the pocket of my jacket. I've piled all my belongings on the chair beside me because I overheated pretty fast. Drinking hot coffee isn't helping.

Ashlynn:
How is it going, did you make it in one piece?

Eve:
Fine, I'm just having my third coffee

Ashlynn:
You'll get wrinkles

Eve:
It'll give me character

Ashlynn:
How was the ride up? You guys are safe?

> **Eve:**
> The roads were pretty clear

> **Ashlynn:**
> It's snowing here again. Is it there?

I look out of the window. There are small flurries but nothing like it came down yesterday. I fill Ashlynn in.

> **Ashlynn:**
> There is bad news about Dash's truck. Leon can't fix it. It needs to go into a garage and have new parts fitted. Actually, he said it might be time to get a new one.

Damn, that isn't good. Cheyenne is a few hours from where we are. I'm not sure if there is an airport nearby that can get him closer to home.

> **Ashlynn:**
> He might have to stay a few days

> **Eve:**
> There is no room at the inn. In case you forgot.

My phone rings. I lean back in the chair and answer the call.
"Holly has been going on about you and Dash leaving together."
"What did you tell her?"
"The truth. She isn't happy."
"It's not like she actually knows Dash."
"That is true. Not as well as you do, anyway."

"Ash, I barely know anything about him."

"You guys didn't talk?"

"Yeah."

"And you like him?"

"Ashlynn, this is all irrelevant. He will be going home today, whether his truck is roadworthy or not. He has a life back in Cheyenne."

"Ha, knew it."

"The first thing you ask someone new is where they're from, it's like talking about the weather."

"That feeling I had this morning, it's getting stronger."

"I'm hanging up."

"Just so you know, two of Carter's friends have agreed to share a room. If need be."

"Not necessary. I'll text you when we're on our way back."

I hang up before she can pass any more of her faux psychic crap on me. She has a fair point though. At least three of our friends have found love with men Ashlynn 'got a feeling' about.

This is not going to happen. We're from different worlds and live thousands of miles away from each other. A darker part of me thinks about Holly and how much she is interested in Dash. Twice now he has walked away from her and come to me.

Not in that way. God, stop letting Ashlynn fill your head with her crap. I need to lay off the coffee. My bladder agrees. I grab my things and head to the restroom, forcing out thoughts of Dash staying longer at the inn.

As I use the bathroom, I hope like hell things are going well up there. I'm not sure what I will say if he comes down looking as miserable as his rivals did.

After washing up, I head back out and see Dash standing in the entrance to the coffee shop, looking around. Oh shit, he must think I left. And we didn't exchange numbers. At least he hasn't been there long. I hurry over and tap his shoulder.

"I thought you got bored and left," he half laughs.

"Restroom," I point to the coffee cups on the table. "How did it go?"

"Okay, I think. I mean they asked a lot of questions. I'm not sure."

"Come on, what does your gut say? You must have got some kind of feeling from them."

"I think you were right about Lewis Henrickson. He was interested in a lot of my ideas."

My smile stretches and he grins back. I hope this isn't a false reaction, and they did genuinely take an interest. I choose to believe he did better than those other people. His passion shines through when he talks about his work.

If he showed even half of that to those people upstairs, then he's on to a winner.

Whether Dash knows it or not, the smile hasn't left his face since he turned to face me.

"This doesn't look good."

I flick up the wipers, so they move faster, clearing the snowflakes. As fast as they sweep away, more land. It's non-stop and has been since we left Evergreen Hollow.

We stopped off at a fast-food place and grabbed something to eat. Dash hadn't eaten due to nerves and was hungry. The sky has gradually grown darker, and Dash commented before it started coming down that the clouds were heavy with snow.

He was right. It's coming down fast, and it's getting harder to see the road ahead of me. I slow down the heavier it starts to fall. Dash reassures me not to worry because the roads are gritted, and the snow tires will keep us on the road.

When we're around ten miles out, I'm really freaking out. He offers to take over and promises not to crash the car or cause me an insurance headache. Feeling safer in his more capable hands, and not trusting my ability to drive in what is starting to become a white out, I relent.

In the short time it takes us to swap seats, I'm shivering and snowflakes cover my hair.

"Ashlynn and her obsession with snow," I grumble.

"You're just not used to the four seasons, living in the southern sunshine," he says, snapping on his belt. He reaches over and brushes something from my hair near my forehead, making me pause in my reply. "Snowflake," he says as a trickle of moisture runs down my cheekbone.

"Oh." I wipe the moisture from my face.

"Seatbelt," he clears his throat.

"Yes sir."

He arches a brow and his lip twitches. Damn, when he does that half smile, he gets a dimple in his cheek.

Dash starts the car, and we set off again. He is a more experienced and careful driver in the snow. What should only take ten minutes, takes almost twenty. When we pull up outside the inn, I let out a sigh of relief we made it in one piece.

Dash glances at his truck. It's been dug out of the snow so the hood could be accessed but has already got a high layer on it again, just not as high as the roof and rear. He frowns at it. I forgot to tell him what Ashlynn said.

He'll find out soon enough, I guess.

"Here," he hands me my hat and I tug it on, then zip up my coat as best I can in the seat. "Be careful when you get out."

I roll my eyes but step carefully out of the SUV. The hotel staff have done what they can to keep the paths clear, but the snow is coming in thick and fast. The wind has really picked up too. I'm thankful for my thick boots with the heavy tread, giving me some traction.

Dash hurries around the front of the car and together we move across the lot towards the steps. This weather is starting to worry me. It was bad on the drive back here, but the snow is pushing up against the foundations of the inn beneath the porch. Whatever the hotel staff have tried to achieve, they're not going to beat mother nature.

I'm beginning to wonder if Ashlynn even checked the weather forecast for this place before everyone came down here. Not that we're going to complain, so far, it's been an absolute blast, but this is different.

I'm starting to worry this could turn into a serious case of being snowed in.

"Shit."

The shout has me spinning around, just in time to watch Dash's arms pinwheeling as he tries not to lose his footing. For a second, I think he's gonna be okay, then his foot slips and down he goes.

"Oh crap," I reach out to try and grab him before he hits the ground.

He lunges for the railing but isn't close enough to stop his ankle turning, forcing him to crash onto the bottom step. His face screws up in pain and he curses.

"Jesus, are you alright?" I bend down so I'm eye level with him and reach out to take his arm.

"That was embarrassing," he grunts. Everything is soaked, his pants, jacket, and shoes. "Stupid fucking shoes."

"Told you, you should have dressed like yourself." He gives me a withering look that screams, not now. "Do you think you can stand?"

Dash rolls onto his knees and uses the step to help push himself up. He curses again as he tries to put weight down on his foot. "I think I turned it," he grimaces.

"It's no good staying out here. Let's get inside and look it over, here," I put an arm around him and help him up the steps. "You're right, stupid fucking shoes," I chuckle, as he almost slips again.

"Don't make this worse than it already is," he tries to laugh but doesn't pull it off. He's in pain and trying not to show it.

"You can lean on me," I tell him as he still tries to put weight on his foot.

"I'm too heavy."

"No, you're not." I maneuver myself so my shoulder is under his arm and grip the back of his jacket. I didn't put my gloves back on so feel the chill from the melting snow on his clothes. "And quit arguing, it's damn cold out here. You need to get this seen to and out of these wet clothes."

"Fuck," he laughs and groans at the same time. "I'm having a really bad couple of days."

"You're tough, I'm sure you can walk it off."

He doesn't answer and I look up at his face as we reach the porch. His skin is white, his eyes pinched. He's putting on a brave face, but this might be more serious than I thought.

I manage to get the door open, and we hobble inside. A man standing by the reception desk spots us and does a double take, then hurries over to help. Together we get Dash to the couch by the window as the man anxiously asks if he is alright.

He's probably worrying about liability. But no one is at fault here. Except for those stupid shoes. The inn can't take the blame for this one.

Dash sits down heavily and leans forward to look at his ankle as the hotel worker hovers. The badge on his uniform reads, Bernard. After staring at Dash for a moment, he straightens and says he is going to get their first aider, before I have a chance to tell him Ashlynn is a nurse.

Taking the spot he vacated, I crouch down and put my hand on the couch next to Dash's thigh. My fingers graze the compact muscle through his dress pants.

He stares at me but anything that might be read into that leaves his expression as he tries to move his ankle.

"Don't do that," I admonish him. "Keep it still. God, your clothes are absolutely soaked."

There is a blanket over the back of the couch which I reach for. I'm pretty sure given normal circumstances he'd refuse, but he's started shivering. I put it over his lap. I'm no nurse but even I can see that doesn't look right.

"How bad is it?"

"Let's just say it's really frigging painful," Dash groans. He leans back and tips his head up to the ceiling, putting one hand over his brow to hide his eyes.

"You're not crying, are you?" I tease.

"Very funny," he peers down his nose at me.

There are no tears I'm pleased to see.

"Maybe we should take the shoe off. It's swelling quite bad, that has got to be hurting."

"Could you?" he asks after leaning forward and realizing he won't be able to do it.

Carefully, I unlace the shoe then gently raise his foot as I slide it off.

"Holy fuck balls. Damn bastard."

"That's creative."

"I'm saying a lot worse inside my head."

Bernard returns with the inn's first aider. She's carrying a first aid box which I'm certain doesn't hold anything that can help. I move out of her way so she can look at the ankle. Immediately she opens the box and takes out an ice pack.

"I'm going to just place this on your ankle," she warns Dash.

"Aaah," he grunts through his teeth.

"I'm sorry."

"It's okay. What's one more freezing thing on my body?"

I stand back and dial Ashlynn's number. I hope she isn't preoccupied with anything. I try to remember the itinerary for the afternoon. Dash and I were gone longer than I intended.

"Are you back?"

"We need you in reception, there's been an accident."

"What kind of accident?" Her voice changes immediately.

"Dash fell over in the snow. I think he might have broken his ankle."

"I'm on my way."

She arrives within a minute, hurrying around the corner from the dining room. Carter isn't far behind. He's a certified EMT too. As are the rest of his firefighter colleagues.

Dash has no idea how lucky he is. Or maybe not given the look on his face as more people appear to see his misery. He tries to tell everyone not to fuss over him, but he needs something more than a tiny ice pack.

I'm sure Dash doesn't want to feel like he's in a fishbowl. These people are family to us. Dash doesn't know any of them. Hell, he barely knows me.

"Nothing to see here, people," Ashlynn gets up. "There is a cake tasting in the dining room right now. Whichever cake gets the most votes is the one we'll use on the big day."

Dash looks up at me with a questioning brow lift. I blink a few times and shake my head. I think he gets the meaning. Don't ask.

Ashlynn pulls the coffee table closer and helps him lift his leg to elevate it. I stand with Carter while she examines him. He winces a lot but tries not to make any sound. No more colorful curses at least.

"I'm happy to say it's not broken. Just a bad sprain. Carter?"

He does a second examination and agrees.

"Just a bad sprain," Dash grumbles and looks up at me. "Can't believe I told you to be careful then I fell on my ass."

"That just means you have a protective nature," Ashlynn smiles.

"How long before I can walk on it?"

"Walk on it?" Ashlynn looks down at him. "You won't be walking on that for a couple of days unaided. The swelling needs to go down. I'm going to get you some ice to help with that for now."

"I can't stay here. I'm supposed to head back home today. It's Christmas in four days."

"Man, have you seen how swollen this is?" Carter adds. "Even if it wasn't the blizzard of the century out there, you wouldn't be driving anywhere right now."

Dash eyes his ankle. I peer around Ashlynn and grimace. It's so swollen now. He won't be able to put any shoes on it as it is.

"A few painkillers and some ice and I'll be good to go. Honestly, I've imposed enough as it is."

Ashlynn and Carter exchange a look. They can't force him to stay. Even I'm not dumb enough to think he can walk on it.

Ashlynn gives me the look next. I pretend not to notice. Especially when I see mischief in her eyes. She is up to something.

Dash looks from her to Carter, then me. He looks confused. I'm confused. What is going on?

Ashlynn puts a hand to her chest and says, in a gentle voice I know for a fact is fake as all hell. "Would this be a bad time to tell you your truck is completely unfixable?"

"What?" Dash's mouth drops open.

Oh, right. *That*.

Chapter 6

A CHEER GOES UP as we climb the stairs. I'm silently fucking fuming. I've already expressed my thoughts on this and all I got in return was a lot of laughter. Fucking firefighters.

As if it isn't embarrassing enough that I fell on my ass. Now this guy is carrying me up the stairs in a fireman's lift.

I don't know where the fuck we're going. It's somewhat impressive how fast he moves, making quick work of the stairs. He lowers me down at the top, at least letting me walk to the room.

Or hobble. Fuck, it's so painful I almost pass out. Eve is following holding the ice pack and my laptop. I've taken some painkillers but they've yet to kick in.

"Where are we going?" I ask Carter. He's still helping me, even though he's set me down.

He brushed over the embarrassment and made no jokes about carrying me, unlike his asshole friends down there.

"Leon and Pat are sharing a room now."

I look over my shoulder at Eve.

"We knew you weren't getting out of here today with that truck," Carter says. "Leon agreed to move. They're roommates already and have twin beds. Don't sweat it."

I'd argue, but I'm starting to feel dizzy. Get it together, the last thing I need is to pass out too.

We enter a room that is on a different corridor to the room I was in last night. Carter holds the door and stands back as I hobble over to the bed and sit down.

"Ashlynn will come back and check on you in a bit but if you need anything just holler."

"Thanks," I mutter. Carter grins and leaves as Eve steps into the room.

"You need to get out of those clothes."

Carter reappears with my bags, winks at Eve and leaves again. These people think of everything.

As well as the pain, I am extremely uncomfortable in the wet clothes. I'll be throwing those fucking shoes in the trash as soon as I can get up.

"Do you need a hand?"

"Is that your way of saying you want to get me out of my clothes?"

"You wish."

I smirk and her cheeks flush slightly. She's right, the damp is seeping into the bedding.

"Just hand me the bag, I'll be okay."

Eve sets my bag down. I unzip it, and rifle through, finding the sweatpants I slept in last night. They'll be the easiest thing to get on. Eve says she will wait outside till I'm changed.

It takes a lot of effort just to get my jacket and shirt off. I toss them to the floor and pull on a Henley shirt. It's warm in here but I'm still shivering. My belt and zipper aren't an issue and I manage to lean on one ass cheek, then the other to get the pants over my hips. When I push them down past my knees, I howl as I accidentally knock my ankle.

The door flies open and Eve rushes in. "What happened?"

She slams to a halt and looks down at my bare legs, my pants around my ankles. And my wet as hell underwear.

Eve clears her throat. "Well, if ever there was a joke about getting caught with your pants down."

"Very funny." I tug my shirt to cover my crotch.

"How are we gonna do this?" she asks, closing the door.

"Do what?" I ask in surprise.

"Well, you need help getting them over your ankle, which is fine with your pants, but your underwear might be a problem, especially with my position."

What the fuck is she talking about? Eve steps close and gets down on her knees.

Oh hell no. Although.... No focus.

"Don't make a big deal about this. Lift your leg."

I'm still trying to get a grip of my shit when her warm hand takes hold of my calf, encouraging me to raise my leg. I stare at the top of her head as she pulls the cuff of the pants carefully over my ankle and slips it off my foot. She drags the other leg down and sets the pants on the floor in a crumpled wet mess.

"I can manage the rest."

She raises her head and looks up at me. I shift on the bed, feeling a stirring where I really don't need it, especially now.

Fucking typical. I haven't had a hard on for anyone in months. Yet sitting here, incapacitated and in soaking underwear, one look from her and it decides to wake up.

Eve goes to the corner and comes back holding a decorative Christmas quilt.

"What do you want me to do with that?" I ask.

"Put it over your lap and take off your undies," she smirks.

"Not a chance."

"You couldn't get your pants over your ankle without help, what makes you think you can get your tighty whities over it."

"They're not tighty whities," I grumble.

"Come on, we're grownups. Pull down your pants."

I cover my face with my hands as Eve laughs.

"If you don't do it, I can always go get Carter to help. Or Holly."

"Fuck no. Just... turn around."

She bites her lip in amusement but turns. I throw the quilt across my lap and with some more grumbling and shifting, get my underwear down. I pull one foot out but wince when I try to do the other without help. Stupid narrow elasticated piece of shit.

"Is it safe to turn around?"

"Yeah," I mutter, tugging the quilt tighter to my body.

Eve makes quick work of removing them and puts them with my pants. She looks up expectantly.

"What?"

"Dry ones. You need me to get it over the foot."

"Jesus Christ."

After rummaging in my bag, I realize I don't have another pair, only the dirty ones from yesterday. I was planning on staying in Evergreen Hollow for one night.

My sister is the kind who always packs 'spares' just in case. Not me. Why don't I listen to her?

"Just help me with the sweatpants."

Eve frowns but must realize why because she stifles another laugh.

"I'm glad this is amusing you."

"I'm only amused by how embarrassed you are. It's not like I'm asking you to lift the quilt."

"Believe me, you wouldn't want that to happen right now," I mutter.

"What?"

"Nothing. Here," I pass her my sweats. She stares at me for a second then gets to putting my pants on me. It hurts when she stretches the elastic over my ankle and I groan, causing her to pause and apologize. She keeps putting her warm hand on my leg and the situation under the quilt is getting dire.

This shouldn't be happening. The pain in my ankle should surely override the blood flow to my damn cock. But nope, it's definitely interested and doesn't care about the pain.

"I got it from here," I tell her, when she pulls my pants up to my knees, where the end of the quilt rests.

Eve uses the bed to push herself up. Despite the absolute mortification I'm feeling, I am grateful. She's done a lot for me today. They all have.

I'm not sure what I'm going to do now. The truck is a massive concern. Not to mention the snow.

"Why don't you get into bed, and I'll go grab anything you might need."

"Sure. Thanks."

"Try not to worry about anything. Ashlynn and Carter don't mind helping you out. I'm sure we can come up with a plan to get you home for Christmas."

I nod. I'm not sure we can but I appreciate her trying. Eve leaves, closing the door. I shove off the quilt and wrangle my pants up, shoving my half hard cock down under the waistband. What kind of sick fuck am I? Who knew pain wouldn't affect my ability to get hard?

God, where the fuck is my head going. I'm delirious. At least I'm dry. But now I need the bathroom. Best to do that before Eve gets back. I really do not want her help to pee.

I manage to get there and back, and my cock to behave before Eve knocks on the door. She has a tray with a drink, a pack of painkillers and a small plate of cookies and chips. She's got a fresh ice pack under her arm.

"Thanks," I say as she sets everything down and carefully places the ice pack on my ankle.

"Do you need anything else?"

"No, I'm good. I'm gonna make some calls and see what I can do about getting out of your way."

She opens her mouth to say something but nods instead. Before she leaves, she gives me her number, telling me to text if I need anything.

My head thumps back on the headboard and I stare up at the ceiling. I'm not a complete idiot, I'm lucky these people have been so nice. I wish like hell I could get out of here. I've barely had time to think about the meeting, let alone call Daria to fill her in on how it went.

The painkillers are starting to kick in. The continual throbbing of my ankle is subsiding. Until I move it, then it hurts again.

After making a few calls and speaking to my sister, it becomes obvious fast that getting out of here in the next couple of days isn't going to happen. The heavy snowfall is forecast to continue for at least another day. After that, there is a possibility I will be able to leave.

I've lined up a mechanic to tow my car, provided he can get to it, and spoken with a couple of rental places who will, weather permitting, be able to get a vehicle to me here at the inn.

Daria is upset, especially about the accident. I distract her by talking about the meeting earlier and how well I thought it went. She is surprised with how I changed up the pitch, but I could hear in her voice too, she is proud.

I guess we're both still not holding out much hope, but at least I did it my way.

She tells me to look on the bright side about everything going on currently. So long as I'm home for Christmas.

The way my luck is going, I'll be lucky to be home for New Year.

The thing with the doors at the inn, you have to manually lock them yourself. Which is a blessing, given every time someone knocks, I don't have to get up, because I haven't locked the door. I'm pretty sure the other guests are trustworthy.

I've slept for a couple of hours between Ashlynn checking in on me, then Carter. Eve comes back a little later. She's changed into a figure hugging black dress with a scoop neck. A heart-shaped pendant is nestled just above the hint of cleavage. She offers to bring me up some food.

I feel like a fucking invalid. Part of me wants to say they should just get on with their wedding celebrations and forget I'm here, but that would make me an asshole. Instead, I politely decline.

"Any word on getting home?" she asks.

"It's a bust. Everywhere I've called has said the weather is too bad."

"That sucks. Hopefully it stops snowing soon and you can at least be home for Christmas."

"That's the plan."

"Okay, well, you have my number," she walks to the door.

My eyes trail to her ass, it's rounded and grabbable and nicely wrapped in that tight dress. My eyes shoot up as she turns back around.

"I feel bad about you being stuck up here. Tonight is just laid back, drinks and food and hanging out. You should come down. And before you say you don't want to intrude, everyone is aware you're up here hiding away. It's making their curiosity escalate."

"I'm not sure I want to be the hot topic in person, Eve."

"It won't be like that. I promise I won't ask Carter to carry you down the stairs."

The look in her eyes is full of amusement. I weigh up the options and decide lying here feeling sorry for myself is stupid. She smiles when I agree. Much to my annoyance, she helps me out of the room and down the stairs.

"I'm starting to rely on you a little too much," I tell her, as we reach the lobby.

"I like having people owe me favors. I won't forget," she winks, and I smile as we head into the bar.

"You came!" Ashlynn cries out and comes over when she sees me.

So much for not drawing attention. She invites me to join their table. I recognize most of the faces.

I get the opportunity to thank Leon for giving me his room. He's chill about it, saying he twisted his ankle once when he landed funny on the pole at work, and knows it's a bummer.

That is a far less embarrassing reason to have turned your ankle.

Like Eve said, everything is more relaxed than the night before. The room isn't packed, people come and go in their own small groups. The biggest group is the firefighters and their partners.

They pay no attention to me, and I wonder if Eve told people to leave me alone. I take a seat and she heads to the bar to get us drinks. I hate her running around after me. She doesn't seem to mind.

"How are you feeling now?" Ashlynn asks.

"The painkillers have taken care of most of the pain. The swelling has gone down a lot too."

"You still need to take it easy."

Carter asks what I'm going to do with the truck, and I explain the calls I've made. Eve returns with a draft beer for me and a glass of wine for her. She takes the seat next to me and immediately begins chatting with the guy to her right. I'm not sure who he is, whether they're related or not. A strange feeling of irritation comes over me.

Ashlyn is smiling when I draw my attention back to her and Carter. I get the feeling she is trouble, especially from the way her and Eve keep having silent conversations.

They involve facial expressions and shifts in body language. I'll never understand how women do that.

As the night goes on, I enjoy chatting with everyone, and then some of the bigger group come to join us. The firefighters are just as I imagine them to be, like brothers who enjoy nothing more than riling each other up.

A hybrid version of truth or dare starts, in that it's all dares. We're all laughing at some of the antics they get up to.

"I'll do it," Chase, one of the younger guy's shouts out of nowhere.

We watch as he starts stripping off his shirt. Eve whoops and I look over at her with narrowed eyes as she covers her mouth behind her hand. When he pulls down his pants too, Ashlynn jumps up to intervene.

Carter is laughing hysterically as the others all egg him on. They trail after him to the front door. Ashlynn is yelling at them to stop being stupid. Those who don't want to go outside hurry to the front windows to watch.

Eve turns to me. "Want to see a naked firefighter in the snow?" she laughs.

"Not particularly."

"What he isn't thinking about," one of his buddies says where he has remained seated. "His nuts are gonna shrink to the size of peanuts. This isn't the flex he thinks it is."

"This isn't a bachelor party!" A shriek comes from the lobby.

"Oops," Eve grins. "Carter's mom will not like this."

"Put your clothes back on *right now*. You *disgusting* man."

Her protests are drowned out by cheering and laughing. Carter holds a hand up to his mom to placate her, but it doesn't work. She's red faced with her anger.

"Sorry, I have to go look," Eve gets up and hurries to the window with some of the others. The guy with me just shakes his head.

"I hope someone takes a picture. We can frame it and put it on the wall at the firehouse."

"Are they always like this?" I ask. Working in construction, being around guys most of the time, I know what it's like when you get a bunch of them together for a few drinks.

"Pretty much." He formally introduces himself as George, the fire station chief and leader of this band of assholes. His words. "They're good guys, they work hard. It's good to see them winding down. Except when they're getting their dicks out."

"You say that like it happens often."

"You'd be surprised," he grunts, making me laugh.

Eve comes back over, grinning. "He's making snow angels in the nude."

"Fucks' sake. Excuse me." George gets up and heads out to break it up, grumbling about the asshole being too sick to work his shifts when they get back.

Carter's mom is still having a meltdown in the lobby as the staff try to wrangle everyone back inside. The snow has slowed but not stopped, and a bracing wind is letting cold air seep into the inn.

"I thought you said tonight would be tame," I say to Eve.

"I forgot about the firefighters," she grabs her wine and finishes it off. "How is the foot?"

"Mixing beer with the painkillers might not be the best of ideas. It feels fine though," I try to move the ankle to prove it and wince. Eve slaps my arm.

"Don't do that. Just because you can't feel it doesn't mean it isn't still healing. The swelling has gone right down," she says leaning down to peer at it. "Nice sock."

"Couldn't get my boot on," I grumble.

"What did you do with the shoes?"

"Kicked them under the bed so I couldn't see them. Trust me, they're going in the trash when I get home."

"You should burn them."

"Don't say that with a bunch of firefighters around."

We both look up at George.

"There is a firepit outside," Eve reasons. "And the best time to set a fire is when you're surrounded by professionals."

"We're not burning my shoes," I shake my head. "Did you get him back inside?"

"Yeah," George points and we look out into the lobby. Chase is covered in blankets in front of the fire. "He'll be lucky if he doesn't get hypothermia, dumb ass."

"He's not used to the snow," Eve says.

"He's an idiot."

We laugh. "I still think we need to have a ceremonial destruction of the shoes."

"Why are you so obsessed with this?" I turn to her.

"And you should burn your tie too, I still have that."

George holds up his hands. "If you want to start a fire in the pit outside, just make sure you have someone there who knows what they're doing."

"That is the only tie I have. I might need it again."

"Come on," Eve nudges me with her elbow.

She's not drunk, but she's had a few glasses of wine over the night. George is right, we shouldn't be starting fires. Although Eve makes a good point too.

Before I know it, she's convinced Ashlynn and a couple of the other women that this is happening. Carter thinks they're nuts but says he'll supervise. I sit, bewildered as Eve goes, with permission, to grab my shoes and tie.

Then we're all gathering on the patio outside, wrapped up in big coats and hats, watching Carter get the fire going. It warms the air considerably once it's fully burning.

"Do you have any words you want to say?" Eve asks me, holding up my shoes.

"Not really," I say dryly.

"Well, allow me. For your crimes against ankles, we ceremonially burn these shoes. Not to mention these shoes very nearly made me fall on my ass when Dash was slipping and sliding everywhere. And as they burn, I hope they know what they did."

She drops the shoes into the fire and sparks fly up making her squeal. Carter pulls her back, even though there is no real danger.

"Wait, the tie," she grabs it from her pocket. A smell like burning rubber starts to fill the space. "With this tie, I plea to the universe to give Dash and his company good luck. And for the panel who interviewed him today to realize he is the best man for the job!"

She throws in the tie. From my seat, I watch as my belongings go up in flames. I'm not entirely sure how I should feel about this turn of events but I'm not mad.

"Oh, that smells so bad," Eve puts a hand over her nose.

"What did you expect burning man-made materials?" Carter laughs.

Everyone starts backing away as black smoke rises from the pit.

"I swear to God you morons should know better. Call yourself professionals," George comes over with a fire extinguisher and puts out the flames.

The acrid smell is almost eye-watering. I've no idea what those shoes were made from. They weren't expensive. I've only worn them a handful of times. People start to hurry inside to get away from it. It's only when I'm hobbling towards the door that Eve comes back out, remembering I need help.

"You're insane," I tell her as she grabs my arm.

"But it's something you'll never forget. And the icing on the Christmas cake will be when you get the contract. You'll be thanking that burning ritual."

She's grinning up at me, the fairy lights highlighting the planes of her face. Her cheeks are rosy from the fire and her hair a mess from the hat she just pulled off. This woman is nuts, but in a good way.

Given the shit time I've had the last couple of days, she's been a bright spot through it all. Everyone here has, but there is something about her.

I didn't need her to burn my shoes for this to be something I will never forget.

Nope, this trip is going to stay in my memory for a long time. Not just for the chance at a job, or the broken-down truck and sprained ankle.

Chapter 7

My head hurts. How many glasses of wine did I drink last night? It didn't seem like that many, but it never does when you're tipsy. This is not supposed to be a boozy vacation.

I remember laughing a lot, and some crazy shit happened. I wince and roll over facing away from the window. Water will help. I'll get up and grab a glass in a minute. Right now, I'm cozy snuggled up in the huge bed. The inn is warm but early morning always has that extra chill to it.

I'll check the weather as soon as I drag myself out of my cocoon.

Did I seriously burn Dash's shoes? He didn't seem annoyed about it, in fact, he went along with it with good humor. A clear image of his face across the fire comes back to me. He was smiling as he watched me.

Even sitting down, halfway incapacitated there was something about him. That henley top hugged every ridge and muscle of his chest and torso. And don't get me started on his shoulders. I have a real thing for big shoulders on a guy. Everything about him is broad and strong, from what I know now is his many years working construction.

He's a man's man in that way, but he isn't gruff or bawdy like some construction workers I've come across in my time.

What am I doing lying in bed thinking about the man in the room next door? He only realized I was in the room beside his after Leon helped him upstairs.

Last night, the temptation to go and check on him was overwhelming. I was just drunk enough that I might ask him something stupid. Like did he need any help getting his pants off? Which I know would hide nothing given he isn't wearing underwear.

Luckily, Holly hadn't come down for the party last night. She had a deadline she needed to work on. I've yet to have a run-in with her about Dash. It's completely unnecessary and there is nothing for her to get mad about, but I know my sister.

She will argue she saw him first. Even though she didn't. I'm not about to get into tit for tat bullshit.

We have a shit load to do today, including the ceremony rehearsal. The rehearsal dinner is tomorrow night before the actual wedding on Christmas Eve. I've also got maid of honor duties I need to get on with. The last two days has been more about enjoying ourselves, being silly.

It's time to get down to business.

Throwing the covers off, I shudder as the cold air hits my bare arms and legs. I grab the throw to wrap around me as I hurry to the bathroom. I start the shower in the claw-foot tub and grab a quick drink of water.

Damn I don't have any painkillers with me. I glance at the wall which backs on to Dash's bedroom. I could always go and ask for some of his. In my tiny sleep shorts and cropped t-shirt, what he would think if I knocked on his door like this.

My nipples are hard in the cold, and I can almost imagine his eyes taking them in. I didn't see much yesterday but from the comment he made and the way he hid himself, I wondered what was going on under that blanket.

Knocking on his door like this is out of the question so I jump in the shower and get dressed. I need to find Ashlynn so we can sit down and get on with some planning.

As I pass Dash's room I hear a thump. The urge to check on him almost takes over but I leave him be. If he needs anything. He'll text. Hopefully. He doesn't seem to be too proud about asking for help. I smother a laugh as I head downstairs, remembering how Carter carried him up the stairs yesterday.

Seeing the look of shock on his face will live rent-free in my head for a while.

There is no sign of Ashlynn in the restaurant, but mom is sitting at a table by herself. I've not spent much time with her since we got here and can't just ignore her now, no matter how much I want to.

Dad text last night to ask how we are. He's been watching the weather forecast and is concerned. About all of us. Mom might not like it, but dad still cares.

"Morning," I say as I stop at the table. "Mind if I sit?"

"Of course not," she waves her hand, and I sit down opposite her.

The servers here are super quick and I have a coffee and have ordered the Santa's bagel sandwich before mom has a chance to say anything. She looks apprehensive. I don't blame her. I haven't exactly been friendly since dad moved out of their house.

"Where's Holly?" I ask.

"She was working late. I didn't want to bother her. I heard about the fire."

Fortunately, there is no lingering smell of burned leather. I laugh it off, not wanting to get into the reasons behind my bright idea last night.

Ashlynn's dad passes and stops to chat for a minute, then heads over to his family at another table.

"It's nice, seeing everyone," I comment.

"Yes, it's been a while since we've all been together. I still can't believe Ashlynn chose a place so out of the way though. Destination weddings are usually at the beach."

"You know how much she loves Christmas."

"Yes, she's always been the same."

"Remember when we had that fake white Christmas. With the fake snow."

Mom nods but doesn't say anything.

Dad did that. He went out and bought a ton of white fabric and boxes to create layered snow. He even got a snow machine, with fake snowmen and Christmas trees.

Ashlynn had never been so happy.

Mom doesn't want to hear anything about it. I'm not going to feel bad about bringing it up. I won't erase dad from my life the way she is. Both have been tight-lipped about the reason for the split.

Holly and I have speculated it's cheating but neither of them is the type, that we know of. We're old enough to understand. It's killing me not knowing.

"Mom, can I ask you something?"

She looks at me with suspicion, but nods.

"I know there is something that you and dad don't want to talk about, but... Ashlynn really wanted him to come. Couldn't you let him?"

"No," she says firmly, her eyes darting away from me.

If I'm not mistaken, something like shame enters her eyes. I'm not sure if it is because she feels bad about telling dad not to come, or if it's to do with their break-up.

"What if he just comes up on the day? Surely you can put aside your differences for Ash's sake?"

Her lips twist and she looks everywhere but at me. "I don't want to talk about this."

"Mom, be reasonable, he's known her as long as you-"

"Eve, I don't want to discuss this," she snaps.

I sit back in my seat as if she struck me. "What the hell happened, mom?"

"It's none of your business. Stop asking me."

People are looking over. I'm not going to get her to admit to anything. All I'm doing is making things more strained between us. This is the wrong place for it.

When we get home, I am going to get to the bottom of this. It can't go on.

"What is going on with the man who had Holly's room the other night? I heard he had an accident yesterday."

So that topic is over. I've started to see this side of her more often lately. She sidesteps conversations all the time. I suppose it's better than yelling and arguing but the whole situation makes me sad. They were so happy for so long, I can't stand seeing this happen.

"Yeah, he fell over and badly sprained his ankle," I say, letting her have her way. "He was supposed to leave yesterday but with that, and the weather, it didn't happen."

"He's lucky he managed to get another room."

"Carter's friends have been great."

"Holly mentioned you went somewhere with him yesterday?" she lifts a brow.

"He needed a ride to the meeting he was in town for. I offered because the car I rented is great for driving in the snow."

"He couldn't have borrowed the car?"

"I didn't get additional driver insurance."

Mom nods and finishes off the last bite of her breakfast. "He's very handsome."

Having learned my lesson yesterday, I glance around the dining room but don't see Dash anywhere. Still, I nod instead of answering, not sure why she is bringing his looks up.

"Typical," she jokes.

"Meaning?"

"Both of you always go for the same man."

"That's not true," I reply.

Mom chuckles. It pisses me off. It's never been the case that we've *gone for the same man*. Holly has tried to take the men I'm with. Or she did before I left for college.

I've barely spoken to my sister since we got here. I should make more of an effort to talk to her. This whole trip is about family after all.

"No one will be going for him, mom. We're here for the wedding and he'll be leaving as soon as the weather changes."

Why does that thought make me sad?

"Morning all!" Ashlynn calls as she enters the dining room. "Big day today. I'm so excited. Is everyone having a good time?"

There are lots of responses and mom goes to give her a hug and then heads back to her room. Ashlynn joins me and we get down to some bride, maid of honor business.

Before I know it, two hours have passed. The wedding planner hasn't been able to make it up here, but she's video calling regularly. Ashlynn goes off to run through things with her and I head upstairs, grab my outer wear and chance going outside.

It has stopped snowing, and the sky is less gray. My eye is drawn to Dash's truck. Most of the cars in the lot are covered in a heavy layer of snow but something about his, pushed over to the side under some bushes, rather than with the rest of the cars, is kind of sad.

The porch rails are also covered with snow. I brush it away so I can lean my elbows on it and look out at the view. It really is gorgeous here. Although I'm not sure I could cope with snow on a regular basis.

Carter wants everyone to go sledding after the rehearsal. I'm not sure if it will go ahead because I don't know the conditions required for sledding. I've never done it before. It should be fun.

A noise behind me catches my attention. Dash is sitting on the bench by the lobby window. He's all wrapped up and looks like he's been there a while. The porch is covered enough that there isn't much snow build up, or the staff have been out and cleared it away.

He's wearing both of his boots and has his phone in his hand.

"I didn't notice you there. How is the foot?"

"I needed some air," he says, then lifts his leg slightly. "It's a lot better today. Got my boot on and managed to walk down the stairs without help."

"Well don't overdo it," I warn.

"I've already been warned," he rolls his eyes.

"Ashlynn?" Dash nods. "It's the nurse in her. Your truck looks kinda pathetic out there."

"I know. The towing company said they could potentially get up here this afternoon to check on it. I'm not holding out much hope. Leon told me about all the things wrong with it."

He sighs and gets up, limping over to the rail to stand beside me. "Not good?"

"I think it's probably time to retire it. It's done me well. I've had that truck since college."

"So, it's ancient then."

"Very funny," he grunts. "I'm not *that* old."

I smother a laugh. "What will you do about getting home?"

"I'm hoping I can get a rental. The weather is calming down so it should be okay. I've had an honorary invite to the wedding. And you'll be glad to hear the staff have done some laundry for me," he adds with a laugh.

The laughter trails off. His eyes lock on mine, and I'm immediately caught up in that stare. My body sways a little towards him. I've never been this instantly attracted to a man before.

Not just his looks. His mind too. I love everything he stands for in his business. The passion he has for it comes across in every word he says.

Mom's words come back to me about how handsome he is. I mean, nothing can happen. He'll be gone tomorrow. I told myself that yesterday too.

Hooking up with a random guy at a family event would be crazy. Right?

Having my mind drawn back to the fact he was rocking the commando look last night isn't where my brain needs to go right now.

"Have you heard about the job?" I ask, breaking whatever spell had come over me.

"Not yet. It'll probably be after the holidays."

"That sucks. Why would they do the meetings now but make you wait that long?"

"They have a lot to think about. They narrowed it down to four companies."

"I'm betting none of them were as good as yours."

He smiles ruefully.

"What is that look?"

"I'm not holding out much hope, Eve."

Why do I like the way he says my name so much? Focus.

"You need to give yourself more credit, Dash. Your ideas are beautiful."

"And expensive."

"Surely, they can afford it. Their company is huge."

"The bigger the business is, the more they want to keep costs down."

"That's a crappy way of looking at it. Why cut corners when you can make something amazing?"

"If only you were on the panel of decision makers. I'd be a shoo-in."

"Think positively," I nudge him.

"In my experience positive thinking never works."

"Are you always this cynical?"

"Never used to be," he mutters, turning till he is side on, resting his hip against the rail.

He shifts his weight to his good leg too and I almost tell him to go inside and rest, but I'm enjoying talking to him. He needs the pep talk too. And maybe he needs something to take his mind off things.

"After the rehearsal, Carter has planned for us to go sledding. The inn provides everything and there are slopes out back. You should come," I glance down. "If your foot is okay."

"I haven't been sledding since I was a kid."

"A hundred years ago?"

"Shut up," he laughs. "What is with the ageism?"

"It's my terrible sense of humor," I cringe but he smiles, he really isn't taking offense. "If it goes ahead and you're still around, you should come."

"Yeah. If I don't manage to get everything sorted."

"Great."

The silence stretches, but it's not uncomfortable.

"Have you been sledding before?" he asks.

"Nope, but I'm looking forward to trying."

"It is fun, especially if you have a snowball fight at the same time. We did that when we were kids."

"I'm sure that's an idea the others would jump all over. You'll have to show us... If you're still here."

"I'm kinda hoping I am now," he says, his voice deepening in a way that has my thighs clenching.

"Me too," I say quietly.

My heart thumps wildly in my chest. It's like a spell has been cast over me. I can't pull my eyes away from him. At least until his drop to my mouth. All I would need to do is go up on my toes and our lips could touch, we're standing that close.

When his eyes rise back to mine, his pupils are completely blown wide. Could he possibly be thinking the same thing?

"There you are."

At the sound of my sister's voice, I take a faltering step back and almost slip. Dash grabs on to my arm and sets me straight.

He leans close. "Try not to sprain your ankle too," he says, his breath tickling my ear.

He's still holding my arm. The energy that was flowing between us earlier comes back with the crackle of electricity. I wish like hell I wasn't wearing a huge coat, so I could feel his touch on my skin.

"Ashlynn needs you," Holly snaps, reminding us she is there.

"Okay," I tell my sister. Her lips are twisted, she looks so much like mom in that moment. Bitter and angry. "Duty calls," I tell Dash.

"Keep me posted on the sleds," he says, releasing my arm.

He limps away before I can leave. I smother my laugh. That was *so* subtle.

"What's going on between you two?" my sister asks.

"Nothing, why?"

"Doesn't look like nothing. You looked two seconds away from jumping him." She narrows her eyes and crosses her arms. I don't want to argue with her about this. She's ruining my good mood.

I shrug instead of answering. What she thinks is not for me to worry about.

Although it isn't so far from the truth.

Chapter 8

The tow company calls to say they can't get up here today but should be alright for tomorrow. Even though Leon said the truck pretty much shit the bed, I want to get a second opinion. I got the same from the rental company, they were struggling for vehicles as people who hired them hadn't had a chance to bring them back yet.

I'm in two minds over whether to be bothered by that or not. I'm not sure what happened between me and Eve earlier, but I was very close to leaning in and taking those perfect lips between mine.

She looked as if she would welcome it.

Until her sister appeared. Knowing what I do about Holly, unfairly or not, I decided to get out of there before Eve left me alone with her.

The wedding party is on the back patio doing a practice run through the ceremony.

I've seen the staff prepping the event room, in case they are forced to come inside. I hadn't realized there was another room. Until I overheard one of the guests lamenting the fact they had to be out in the cold, when there is a perfectly good room indoors. Ashlynn really has her heart set on doing it out there.

I brought my laptop down and sat in the dining room to work. I don't have a clear view of everything going on but do see some of it.

Eve is standing beside Ashlynn, who is facing Carter, while the officiant talks. I've always wondered why people practice wedding ceremonies beforehand. Surely, it's fairly obvious how it works.

I've been to enough weddings, seen them on TV, to know how it goes. It also feels like it's taking some of the magic out of the actual event.

As I watch, Eve's head turns, and she spots me in the dining room. Her lip lifts slightly, as though she wants to smile, but not let anyone know she's being distracted. By me.

Getting married has never been on my radar. If I'm honest, I would like a family, one day. I need to get my shit in order first. With a company on the verge of folding because work has dried up, this is not the time to think about settling down.

I'd have to meet someone I thought I could spend my life with first.

My attention goes back to the group outside. Everyone is laughing at something. Eve's head is thrown back, and she's clutching her stomach. God knows what has them all hysterical. I can't help but smile watching her.

The restaurant staff bring food out and set it up on a long table. It smells delicious. It's not for me though. I carry on answering emails and searching for other jobs we can take on if this thing with the hotel falls through. This time of year is notoriously difficult to find work. People are shutting down for the holidays.

When everyone starts trickling in, I've sent messages to three companies I've done some work for before. And reached out to a few new ones.

"Let me just go ask the staff what they think," Carter says as he walks in ahead of the others. He spots me and pauses. "Actually, Dash you're from around here, right?"

"Not around here," I say in confusion.

"I mean the state, you're used to snow like this right?"

"Sure."

I close the lid on the laptop as other people start coming inside, taking off their outer layers and heading for the warm food and drinks.

"Could you come check the snow for us? I mean it looks good to me, we used to go sledding in Big Bear Lake when we were kids. Ashlynn wants someone *who knows*," he makes finger quotes. "To check it's safe."

I agree and grab my coat from the back of my chair.

"You good on that ankle?" Carter asks.

"I'm good."

It's not perfect, but it's much easier to walk, so long as I don't go far, or put too much weight on it.

Carter slaps my shoulder. We step off the back porch and walk out onto the land at the rear of the inn. The slopes aren't too steep, and from what I can see, there are no real obstacles.

There has been a lot of heavy snowfall over the last few days. More than a good few inches has settled. It's still wet, and heavy and looks packed enough. It's not too deep to walk in either, my boots aren't sinking too far. I nod at Carter.

"You should be good. What kind of sleds do you have?"

"Wooden ones, with skis."

"You'll definitely be okay with them."

"Great, I'll let the others know. Eve mentioned something about snowball sledding?"

I laugh and explain what my family used to do when we were kids.

"That is an awesome idea. There are people who don't want to sled but I don't see why they can't start making us snowballs. You think you can join in?" he asks. "With your ankle?"

"It's still a little tender. I'm not sure I'd be able to control a sled, especially braking."

"You can share with someone. Or do what we did when we were kids and just fling yourself off it if it's going too fast," he laughs. "You're welcome to join."

"Thanks man, appreciate that. If I can't sled, I can make snowballs like a pro."

"Good man," he slaps my shoulder again.

A little over half an hour later, those that want to sled are outside, ready to go. They're going with the snowball sledding idea. I've spent twenty minutes making a mountain of snowballs with some of the people who don't want to sled but want to enjoy the snow. Most of the younger ones have thrown as many as they've made. Everyone is having fun.

I'm stacking up another pile when a snowball hits me in the back of my shoulder. I straighten and spin around to see Eve laughing.

"Seriously?" I shout to her.

She pulls her hand from behind her back, launching another one at me. I manage to duck out of the way, it sails over my head. Her hands are empty now. Big mistake. I lunge forward and grab three snowballs and stand up.

Her eyes widen when she sees my arsenal. She spins to run away as I throw one. I don't put as much as I can into the throw, because I don't want to hurt her. My aim is true though, and it smacks her right in the lower back. She cries out and turns around, just as I toss another one which hits her chest.

"Stop," she shouts through her laughter. Then drops to her knees to make more balls.

"You shouldn't pick a fight when you don't have enough ammo," I yell over to her. "That's the first rule of a snowball fight."

She throws her half assed attempt at me, but it falls apart in mid-air and drops uselessly to the ground. I wind up to throw another and she turns and just runs. My throw completely misses.

"Picking a fight with a guy who can't run helps!"

"Damn, you wound me."

A snowball flies out of nowhere and hits her in the neck. Eve screams as the snow gets inside her coat. I glance behind me to see Ashlynn grinning as she walks towards me, holding out her hand. I high five her.

"You traitor," Eve yells at her cousin.

Just as Ashlynn smashes a snowball on the top of my head.

"Ah fuck," I hold my hands up to brush the snow from the back of my neck, but some of it goes down my shirt, anyway. "That was cold."

"It's snow."

"I meant the attack."

"It's every man for himself." She's grinning wildly until someone hits *her* with one, and she shouts in surprise.

"Who the hell threw a snowball at my wife!" Carter yells

"Wife," Ashlynn puts a hand to her chest and gives her fiancée a goofy grin.

"*You* did it!" Eve calls, walking toward us.

"Me?" Carter looks around. "I would never…"

He pulls another snowball out and turns to throw it at Eve but she's somehow managed to make a couple of her own. She throws both of them, one after the other. One hits Carter right in the face, the second hits south of his abdomen.

"Aah, my balls," he cries and drops to his knees.

"Eve!" Ashlynn yells, crouching down to check on Carter.

"Sorry," Eve calls, not sounding sorry at all.

"Good throw," I tell her as she gets closer.

"Dude," Carter wheezes. "You're supposed to be on my side."

"Are you okay?" Ashlynn asks in concern.

"Nothing you can't fix babe," he grabs for Ashlynn, pulling her down. He pushes her onto her back and presses kisses all over her face and neck.

"Gross," Eve wrinkles her nose. "Get a room."

A few other people start cheering and whistling till Carter stands and helps Ashlynn up. She buries her face in his neck, and he kisses the top of her hair. They're both covered in snow but don't seem to mind.

Eve is watching them with a soft smile on her lips.

She catches me looking. I don't turn away and she doesn't lose her smile.

Carter calls for attention and the inn's staff bring out the sleds. There are eight sleds which will race down the slopes while lobbing snowballs at each other. The aim of the game is to knock your opponent off balance and be first to reach the finish line.

I've never seen a group of people organize a professional-looking competition so quickly.

It sounds absolutely fucking crazy. And awesome. I'm kinda bummed I can't do it too. There aren't many people who want to take part, saying they just want to sled and will do it after this insane game.

It ends up with an uneven number, which means one team will be a man down.

"Dash, you think you can do it?" Leon calls. "I heard this was your idea man, you should take part."

It will be crazy to do it with this injury.

"You can ride on back and be the thrower," Eve steps up. "I can steer the sled."

"You want me ride with you?" I ask.

"What, you don't think I can drive a sled?"

"You've never driven a sled in your life."

"I'm a fast learner."

I turn to Carter. "I think there should be some practice runs before you commence with the snowballs."

"That's probably a good idea," he says.

"So you'll do it?" Eve comes over. "You can teach me how to drive this thing. Then with my skills on the sled and your snowball expertise, we can take these guys on and win."

"You're only asking him to ride with you because he's probably the most experienced one here," another woman calls. I think she is one of the bridesmaids.

"And cos he's cute," another one shouts.

"Hell yeah," Ashlynn whoops.

"Fucking hell," I groan, putting my hands on my hips and looking at the floor, a little embarrassed.

Eve is laughing.

"Wait, what's the prize? If we win, what do we get?" Chase, the naked snow angel firefighter yells.

"Five hundred bucks to the couple who win," Carter answers.

I look up at him in surprise. No one else seems fazed by that. Five hundred dollars would be pretty good right now. Or two fifty, given I'd split it with Eve.

"Do I see a competitive side coming out there," Eve steps closer. "You should know, I hate to lose."

"Is that so?"

"Yeah. If you think your ankle is okay, what do you say? Want to be my partner and beat these assholes?"

"Hell yes."

"Remember your only job is to keep us straight. As much as possible. That will make it easier for me to aim."

"Got it," Eve nods.

We've practiced on the slope for half an hour. There has been a lot of laughing and a lot of falling off. And not just from us. My ankle hasn't been too bad, but that is probably because it's cold as hell and the snow is acting as a natural ice pack.

Eve is a quick learner and got the hang of the sled quickly. We've spent the whole time we've been making our snowballs, strategizing on how we're going to take out our opponents.

George, the fire chief has agreed to be the referee, slash judge. Along the slope racetrack, they've positioned people they're calling counters. Those who can keep track of any snowball hits.

It's so organized it's like they've been doing this for years. The firefighters work together like a well-oiled machine. There are heats, a quarter and semifinal, before the final two battle it out. Someone has even drawn up a score sheet. Ashlynn's mom is sitting on the patio, covered in a blanket, ready to note down each race winner.

As the races get under way, I stand close to Eve watching our competition. I point out where they're going wrong and who we need to watch out for. Eve is bouncing on her toes, her gloved fists clenched, psyching herself up.

The first race is a draw, only two hits each because they're lobbing the balls all over the place. The drivers aren't that experienced, but they're in hysterics as they crash to a stop at the bottom.

Then there is another team who are fucking amazing and land seven balls, while their competitor hits none. They make the walk of shame but some of the older ladies have warm spiced cider or mulled wine waiting for them.

When it's our turn, we run over our tactics as I load up my balls. "You sure you can drive."

"If you have no faith in me, then we're already screwed," she pokes me in the chest.

"I have faith. We got this."

"Damn right we do."

Eve gets onto the front of the sled, and I slide on behind her, my thighs wrapping around hers. I've made a sling out of a scarf which is holding the snowballs in my lap. We kept that hidden from everyone else. Most of the other teams have been dropping more than they've thrown.

I can't help but laugh when Eve glares at our opposition. "Your toast," she says.

"Bring it Dalton."

"Eat my snow," she faces front. "Aim for the head," she whispers to me.

"You're gonna kill me if we lose, aren't you?"

"We're not gonna lose."

And we don't. In fact, in our first race, the other team both fall off halfway down. I manage to land three balls before they wiped themselves out. Our second race is close, but we manage to get two hits more by the time we reach the bottom.

A few times I've had to grab hold of Eve when she's gone a little wild with her over steer. She's been screaming and laughing and shouting obscenities at people on all our races. And I love every second of it.

We reach the semifinals and there is a lot of trash talk going on at the top of the slopes. The more packed the snow is getting from all the sleds, the faster they're racing down them.

"May the best team win," Carter shakes my hand, then Eve's. "Us," he adds.

Ashlynn rolls her eyes. Carter is driving their sled, while Ashlynn throws. She's good. Eve said she was a pitcher on the junior varsity baseball team in middle school. They're going to be tough to beat.

Strike that, we can beat them.

George starts the race and we're pushed off, I immediately start launching balls. I aim for Carter though, not wanting to hit Ashlynn. Also, I figure if I can knock the person steering the sled off, then we've got more chance of winning.

A snowball hits me hard to the side of the head. It feels like I got hit by a baseball bat. "Ow, fuck."

"Are you okay?" Eve shouts and looks back over her shoulder. Her body leans and the sled follows the movement. We start to careen sideways.

I grab her hips and pull her back into me, gripping hold of her and leaning the other way. Our combined weight straightens us up, but the sled judders. We're getting pelted by snowballs and they're overtaking us.

"No!" Eve shouts.

It's clear as day to me we're going to lose control. I wrap my arms around her middle as the sled starts to tilt, going up in the air on one side. I flip us off, so we roll away from the sled, landing in the snow. Doing my best to shield her from getting hurt, I hit the snow first. It's fresh snow and we sink into it rather than slam down.

We come to a stop with me on my back and Eve on top of me. My arms are still wrapped around her middle, her back to my chest. Our coats are padded enough that her lying on top of me doesn't hurt. The wind is knocked out of me though.

"Are you okay?" I ask her.

"No," she moans.

Easing her off me so she is on her back, I prop myself up to look her over, searching for any injuries.

"We lost," she groans. "I can't believe we got so close."

"Wait, you're not hurt?"

"No," Eve finally looks up at me. "Are you?"

"I'm good. I think."

"God, I can't believe I messed up."

"It was my fault, I put you off. But she hit me right in my ear. It stings like hell."

I reach up to rub my ear. At the bottom of the slope, Ashlynn and Carter get off the sled and jump into each other's arms.

Eve lifts her head to watch then drops it back into the snow with another groan.

"At least it was the bride and groom who beat us."

"That makes it worse, Dash." She closes her eyes.

Stifling a laugh, I look her over. "Are you sure you're not hurt?" I ask again.

Her blue eyes pop open and she looks up at me. Her nod is subtle. Her hat is askew and her blonde hair is spilled out in the snow. My body is still over hers, one hand at the side of her head.

Eve reaches up and brushes the snow out of my hair over my ear.

"Does it really hurt?"

My ear is throbbing but I don't say anything. Vaguely I can hear people cheering at the bottom of the slope. We're the only ones still up here. Her chest is rising and falling as she stares at me. Her hand lingers in my hair, her fingertips trailing over the shell of my ear, down to my lobe.

If ever there was a signal, this is it, right? Fuck, her lips look enticing right now, especially when they part slightly. Without questioning it, I lower my face closer to hers. Her fingers move to the back of my head, gliding through my hair.

Closing the distance, my lips meet hers. She lets out a soft moan. Desire flares through me, as Eve raises her head slightly, and deepens the kiss. Her lip's part and I take it as an invitation, my tongue teases hers for just a moment before I pull back.

She lets out a shaky breath, our eyes locked on each other, our breath mingling. Nothing going on around us matters right now. I want to dive back in, I want to take her lips again and again. Fuck, I want to do more than that.

"Eve, Dash, are you alive!"

Fuck. I pull back and rest on my knees. Ashlynn is hurrying up the slope, coming into sight as I take Eve's hand and pull her into a sitting position. She continues to stare at me until Ashlynn reaches us.

She looks between the two of us and arches a brow.

"Nice hit," I tell her, brushing snow off my gloves and leaning back on my haunches.

Eve rolls up and gets to her feet.

"Don't be a sore loser, Evie," Ashlynn says, nudging her cousin.

Eve pouts but after a few moments concedes the win. Getting to my feet I glance between the two women as they both look back at me.

"Come on down, we're gonna have a quick hot cider before the final. I mean, unless you guys need some space."

Eve rolls her eyes. "Alcohol sounds amazing."

She resets her hat and starts down the slope. Ashlynn checks on my ankle but it's fine.

I can't get that kiss out of my head. What the shitting hell am I thinking, kissing her like that? I know damn fine and well what it is.

As I follow, Eve looks over her shoulder at me, and something crackles in the air between us.

All I can think about is doing that again. And a lot more. She smiles at me then turns away. I really wish her entire family weren't waiting at the bottom of that hill for us.

Especially since they're giving us shit for wiping out.

And my cock is hard as steel.

Chapter 9

Eve

We watch the final race, Dash standing with some friends of Carter's. I stay with Ashlyn's parents. I'm convinced my other aunt and uncle, who made it to the final, let Carter and Ashlynn win.

There is a brief ceremony at the end where Carter announces he will donate the five hundred dollars to a charity the firehouse has been supporting. He really is the perfect guy.

We have some spiced cider by the fire on the patio. It's been cleared out and there is no longer a smell of burned leather coming from the stone pit.

Dash is with a few of my cousins now, laughing about how we ended up losing. They're telling him they were sure we were going to win, and I get pissed all over again. I wanted to win.

It was all my fault. Dash is a grown up, he could handle a snowball to the head.

I was too busy worrying about whether he was okay. And... then, well. What happened after.

It's hard not to watch him as he laughs and drinks with my family. Not after that kiss. It wasn't completely unexpected. In fact, I've been thinking about what it would be like to kiss him for ages. He didn't disappoint. It wasn't a long kiss, barely lasting more than a few seconds. It wasn't just the kiss that was making me feel all tingly.

It was the anticipation of it, the thump of my heart, and between my legs as he stared at me. The painfully slow movement as he dipped his head to mine and our lips touched. Everything about it was perfect and a really bad idea.

He's leaving tomorrow. Probably. No matter what I feel about that kiss, the chances are I'll never see him again after today. The more I watch him, the harder it becomes to convince myself I shouldn't take it any further. A few times, he's caught my eye. I want to know what he is thinking about.

It's time to take a break from all the noise and people.

Ashlynn hounds me into my room and closes the door, leaning back against it. My eyes roll as I kick off my wet boots and hang my coat up on a chair. She's waiting. Well, I'm stubborn and can wait just as long as she can.

I'm not sure how much she saw, but she knows something happened. My hat is tossed on top of the jacket, and I walk to the mirror to look at my hair. It's a mess. Using my fingertips I comb out the knots and wet patches. In the reflection I see her staring at me. Her arms are folded, one finger tapping against her forearm.

"What?" I ask innocently.

"Don't you *what* me. I know what I saw. Now spill."

"If you know what you saw, why are you asking?"

She slinks over to the bed, kicks off her boots and sits cross-legged in the middle of it. "Eve, did you kiss him?"

"Ssh," I hold up my hands.

"Why?"

"His room is next door."

"He was still downstairs when we left."

"He might have come up, and the walls are thin."

"Are they?" she frowns.

"Yes, so whoever is in the room next to you guys should probably get earplugs."

"Your neighbors could need them too," she fires back. Then looks around. "Although you have a corner room and his is next door, so if he came in here, technically no one would hear."

"Oh my God, stop."

"Why, he's hot. And no offence, but you need to get laid."

"Life doesn't revolve around sex."

"Doesn't it?"

I throw my hairbrush at her. It was never going to hit her, but she flinches anyway.

"You're with the love of your life, you're happy and you live together. Sex on tap is normal for you. You know I don't do one-night stands, Ash. I need a connection to have sex with someone."

"I'm sorry but I've seen the connection bouncing between the two of you," she picks up the brush and toys with it. "He watches you all the time."

"How would you know that? You're in your room having all the sex."

She laughs again then pats the bed. "Come, sit with me."

I roll my eyes but move, sitting cross-legged facing her. We used to do this all the time when we were teenagers. Talking about school and boys and make-up and all the other inconsequential shit you talk about when you're a kid.

"Who kissed who?"

I twist my lips and think back on the kiss. "Him. He made the first move. He leaned in first..."

"So he clearly wants you."

"Wait... I was touching his hair. You threw a snowball and his ear was stinging."

She makes an 'o' shape with her mouth and slaps my thigh. "*You* made the first move," she pokes my knee.

"I was trying to see if he was hurt. Not seducing him."

"You gave him a signal, and he went for it, because he *likes* you. Come on girl, you know he sets your underwear alight."

A laugh bursts out of me.

"How long has it been, anyway? Since Vance? That asshole. Are there cobwebs down there?"

I don't answer because those are stupid questions. And she's right about my ex. He was the last man I was with. I haven't actively steered clear of men, I just haven't met anyone I wanted to take things further with. I do need to feel a connection. It's a me thing.

"All I'm saying is, what is the harm in taking a small risk and having some fun?"

"When are we supposed to do this? You want me to just go knock on his door and invite him here?" She shrugs as if that isn't a bad idea. "This place is filled with family. You want me to have a one-night stand with all of them around us?"

"We're not going to be lining up to watch."

"Ew."

"Stop making excuses."

"Stop trying to force me to have sex with him."

"No one is forcing you, Eve," she takes my hand. "I just think he'll be good for you. Even if it is just for one night. He's a genuinely nice guy. He's been gracious, he's offered to pay for the room, and he's helped Carter out with some things."

"He has?"

"Yeah. Not to mention he is damn fine. Did you notice the other night when he was wearing sweatpants that he was," she leans in and puts a hand around her mouth. "Swinging free."

My mouth drops open. Yeah, I did notice. In fact, I knew without a shadow of a doubt he didn't have underwear on, because I helped him put those sweatpants on. All the while knowing he was naked under that quilt.

What I want to know is why she noticed.

"Why were you looking at his crotch?" I whisper shout.

Ashlynn smirks. God, if she is trying to get a rise out of me, it worked.

"It's a shame really that he lives all the way out here."

"Make up your mind, Ash. Are we having a holiday fling or a long-distance relationship, in the world according to Ashlynn."

"All I'm saying is, go with the flow. Don't rule it out. Just see what happens."

"You're delusional. He might not want to sleep with me."

"Now who's delusional?" She gets off the bed. "Jenny is going to do our make-up and hair trial later. So…"

"So what?"

"Just saying, it might be a good time to dress to impress."

Choosing to believe Dash isn't that shallow, I change into leggings and a sweater. My hair and make-up look phenomenal, but in a natural way. Ashlynn got emotional when she saw us bridesmaids in our dresses. Thank God we all still fit in them because we would have been screwed if we didn't.

Ashlynn didn't put her dress on. She says it's bad luck.

"I can't believe there is only two more days till the wedding," Helene says.

She's Carter's only sister and one of the bridesmaids. We're sitting in the bar which is relatively quiet by the last few days standards. The guys have left us alone for the most part, probably because Ashlynn told Carter this was her afternoon and evening with her girls.

"I know, I wish it would hurry up already."

We laugh at how excited she is. Ashlynn was born to be married. Luckily, when her crappy ex proposed as a way to win her back, she turned him down with a resounding 'go to hell'.

"I just want to say that I don't think my brother could have found a more perfect person to spend his life with," Helene says, reaching for her champagne glass. She leans in closer and half whispers. "No matter what my mother thinks."

Everyone laughs but Ashlynn's smile doesn't reach her eyes.

It kills her that Carter's mom has been less than welcoming to her. She wants her to like and approve of her. I've told her more than once that the only person who counts is Carter and he adores her.

The woman is going to be in Ashlynn's life. She is constantly worried she is going to say or do something to offend her.

There isn't a very long list of things that don't offend her. I've steered clear. The others have talked about some of the shit she's tried to pull, and her disdain for the inn. She even said if it wasn't snowing so heavily, she would have found somewhere else to stay.

"All that matters is Ashlynn and Carter were made for one another," I say, drawing the attention away from her soon to be mother-in-law. "And you guys are going to have the most amazing life together. I'm so happy for you."

"Thanks," Ashlynn sniffles, her eyes welling with tears. "He is perfect." She shakes it off and lifts her glass, we all follow. "To finding the perfect man," she says, her eyes sliding to me and a brow lifting as we all repeat the toast.

Over the course of the night, I can't stop myself from thinking about Dash. He hasn't come down so far this evening. I begin to doubt myself.

What if he regrets the kiss and is avoiding me? Ashlynn and her *feeling* are broken.

Trying not to let it get me down, I laugh and joke with my family and friends. What's to be let down about? It's not like we're dating or even anywhere close to it. Maybe there is a mutual attraction there. It's not meant to be acted on. Wrong place, wrong time.

Dash is a sensible guy, with a lot on his plate. He probably sees me as another complication on top of everything going on for him right now. It's irrational to be hurt.

Doesn't stop me feeling stupid over that kiss. I did instigate it, maybe he got caught up in the moment and realized it was a mistake.

It's getting late, so I decide to turn in. Ashlynn is preoccupied so I let her be, not wanting to bring her good mood down. As I head out to the lobby, I notice someone walking down the hallway to the event room.

It's Dash. What is he doing?

There is nothing down there except the room we might end up using for the ceremony. It's not off limits per se, but no one goes down there, especially at night.

I doubt he is up to no good. It just seems weird. I should leave it alone and go to bed. If he wanted to talk to me, he would have come into the bar. My curiosity is piqued.

Making a snap decision, I follow him.

The door to the room is slightly ajar. I step up to it and peer inside. Dash is standing in the middle of the room with his hands in his pockets, staring at the floor.

The room itself has been decorated in preparation for being a back-up. The same color scheme, decorations and a perfect Christmas tree are all ready and waiting. The only light in the room is from the lights on the tree and the lamps outside the windows.

What is he doing?

The door creaks as I accidentally brush against it. Dash turns around.

"Hey. What are you doing in here?" I ask, deciding not to try to hide, which I couldn't pull off considering he's looking right at me.

"I wanted to go somewhere quiet. Everywhere else is busy. And the lady in the room next to mine was arguing with someone."

"Really?" I'm not sure who is in the room next to him, or why they'd be arguing.

"She was on the phone," he adds. "Unless the person she was arguing with sat there and took it. Or whispered," he frowns. "Sorry."

Who is in the room next to him? It could be Carter's mom. Maybe she was yelling at her husband. He seems the type to sit quietly and take it. I consider asking what they were arguing about but leave it. That isn't why I'm standing here.

"Want me to go tell them to keep it down?"

"Nah," he answers. "It gave me an excuse to get out of the room."

He walks to one of the decorated chairs and sits down.

Something is wrong. Oh no. What if he got *the call*?

I move into the room and close the door. He might not want to talk about it, especially if it's what I think it is. Dash looks up as I take a seat across the aisle from him.

"You should go back to the party."

"I was on my way to my room when I saw you come down here. If you want me to leave..."

I trail off. I can't force him to tell me what is wrong. Offering silent support is all I can do. If he doesn't want to take me up on it, I'll go.

We sit in silence for a moment. Dash lets out a huffing laugh. "Lewis Henrickson called."

"What did he say?" I lean forward on the chair. He doesn't need to remind me who that is.

Dash clasps his hands together between his knees and stares at them for a moment. When he looks up, he is so dejected, I already know the answer. My heart breaks a little.

"It's not as bad as you think. Although I'm beginning to think it's worse than a straight up no."

My brow creases. "What does that mean?"

"He wants me."

"That's great."

"The others don't."

"Oh."

"Yeah... And right now, he isn't the biggest shareholder in the company."

"I don't understand."

Dash looks up at me. "He said he loved my ideas, said it's his dream project but his dad and uncle are stuck in their ways. They can't see as far ahead as he can, or the appeal of a building like mine. They've been arguing over it. But it's looking more like they're going to go with someone else."

"They're idiots. At least you got some good feedback. Like Lewis said, they've not made a decision yet. It sounds like he is going to fight for it."

He gives a rueful smile. "He's out numbered, Eve. I always knew it was a long shot. Environmentally friendly construction isn't as advanced as I would like it to be."

"But it's such a huge thing. People all over the world are doing everything they can to make things more eco-friendly, and sustainable for the future of the planet."

"It's the one place where big construction falls down. Especially with guys like the Henrickson's. It is a growing business, and there are a lot of good properties being built. It's just not as mainstream as you would hope."

"I'm sorry."

Dash shrugs. "Like I said, it was always a longshot. I've never done anything that big before. It's not just the environmental aspect. It's my reputation in such a big arena, or lack thereof," he adds wryly. "There are a lot of other factors. The only saving grace is Devon Bright aren't the company they're interested in. At least I was considered a legitimate option over those assholes."

It's a small win but irrelevant really.

"You're still not out of the running. He didn't call to tell you no."

"It was a preemptive courtesy, Eve."

"You don't know that. He might talk them round."

"I appreciate the optimism."

"You can't give up."

"What else should I do?" He asks, leaning back in his chair. His face is contorted in an angry frown.

It's not directed at me. Frustration is emanating from him in waves. I can't help but remember him saying this is the biggest meeting of his life. Or forget the lengths he went to, to get to the meeting.

This is serious. And he's stuck here, with all of us. Not with his family, or his business partner.

I wonder if he has told her yet. My guess is not. He probably wants to spare her the disappointment so close to Christmas. It irritates me Henrickson didn't give Dash the same grace.

He might have thought it was a courtesy. Calling to tell someone how great they think they are but they're not going to get the job is a dick move. No matter what he thought he was doing by telling him.

You're great, but not what we want right now. Who does that?

It would have been better not to give him a kernel of hope. Not that Dash believes he has any hope. All he can see is he lost the opportunity.

As I've sat here thinking, his frustration has turned to guilt. It's written all over his face, in the stoop of his shoulders. He is taking all of this on those broad shoulders of his and it's not fair.

"Hey," I walk to his side of the aisle, taking a seat in the row behind his so I'm right next to him. I touch his elbow. "You can't blame yourself."

"The company is my responsibility."

"You have a business partner."

"I'm not putting any of this on my sister." He looks at me like I'm crazy.

"So why would you put it on yourself? She worked as hard as you did. You both put everything into this equally. How is it your fault and not hers?"

"I'm the CEO. I'm the one who takes the blame."

"There is no blame here, Dash. This is backwards thinking and stupidity on the part of the idiots building this hotel. You could have gone in there with the building of the century, and they wouldn't have chosen you."

"Way to make me feel better."

"You know what I mean. You just don't want to admit that this is on them. Not you. I get it. You're the face of the company, the one putting yourself out there, but you can't take the blame for this."

"You don't understand."

Maybe I'm starting to. He had everything riding on this. I know what it's like, owning your own business, struggling to keep work coming in. I'm lucky enough to have a great client base, something that is ongoing with each one. Construction is a one and done kind of business.

Sure, you get word-of-mouth recommendations and other people come looking for you. It's not always that simple.

Taking a chance, I ask the question that most other people in my situation would avoid like the plague. Regardless of what Ashlynn thinks is a sexual attraction between us, there has been some kind of bond. It might not be the next big friendship of my life, or even a romantic one, but I am invested. And I want to help if I can.

"How bad is it?"

Dash gets up and walks to the window. Shit, maybe I'm wrong. I almost get up and run away but he starts to talk before I do, showing he trusts me. And that keeps me rooted to my seat.

"It was the last chance I had to stop my company going under."

Chapter 10

The snow is coming down again. In soft flurries, not the heavy snowfall of the last few days. It's the kind of snow that wouldn't stick, if there wasn't already a good few inches of it piled up out there.

I get what Eve is saying. The phone call wasn't an outright no. I'm not stupid. No matter how much Lewis Henrickson likes my designs, they're never going to go for it.

I've run through the gamut of emotions since the phone call. Disappointment, sadness, anger, bitterness. Then the guilt brought up the rear with the speed of a freight train.

What if I'd made a mistake changing my pitch up? That really fucks with my head. I am so angry with myself, which pisses me off even more because I went in there and laid out my heart and soul.

I shouldn't feel bad about that.

At the end of the day, I was myself. If it cost me the job, I can at least hold my head high for being authentic. There is no point regretting it.

Eve has been silent since that stupid declaration. I had no intention of telling her how dire my situation is. I mean, it's not actually that bad. I've heard back from a couple of people I reached out to. They have some work for me after the holidays. It's not an enormous amount of money. Or particularly interesting. If building a parking garage can keep food on my sister's table, that is all that matters.

The scent of her alerts me she is close. Eve steps up beside me and stares out of the window too. We watch the snow fall together.

"I feel bad for burning your one and only tie."

Caught off guard by that, I laugh. It's a fucking odd thing to say at a moment like this, after telling her my business is about to go up in flames. Turns out it is just what I need to hear.

Eve laughs with me. She turns and leans her shoulder against the wall by the window.

"In all seriousness," she says. "Having seen your designs, I don't think it will be too long before more people come knocking. And who knows, once those stuffy old bastards retire to their super yachts and mansions, Lewis might reach out."

"I appreciate the sentiment. It doesn't solve my current situation."

"No, it doesn't. Tequila might help."

I smirk. "Alcohol never fixed anything."

"True, but it can make you forget for a little while."

"I've never been the type to run away from my problems."

"You know, I get that about you."

"Yeah?" I turn and lean my shoulder against the wall too, on the other side of the window, facing her. "What makes you think that?"

"Everything you've had to deal with since you showed up here. You could have got out of this situation in so many ways. I could have dropped you off in Evergreen Hollow where you probably could have got home from. You came back here. For that ancient truck of yours. Which is not likely to start again."

"That's hardly something to be proud of. If anything, it's kinda pathetic."

"I don't think so. It shows character. You could have dumped the truck and made it the Inn's problem. Integrity is something a lot of people are lacking these days."

I've never known someone for such a short amount of time, have so much belief in me. In the last three days here, I've laughed more than I have in weeks. It's not all down to Eve but she's been a huge part of it.

What is it about her? She hasn't just made me laugh, she's made me feel something else too. A spark of desire, of something more than the existence I've been living, trying to make my business work. Fighting for everyone I employ, for my sister. Taking on that burden.

I've done nothing for myself lately. What I'm about to do is crazy. She might tell me to fuck off but given our previous kiss, I'm inclined to think she won't.

Maybe. Hopefully. I take the few short steps between us, closing the distance. Eve's chin tilts up and I watch her pulse thump in her neck. It's fast, almost in rhythm with my heartbeat. She doesn't tell me to back off.

So I don't. I wrap an arm around her waist and pull her to me, then lock my lips down on hers. She lets out a surprised whimper but doesn't push me away. Instead, she grabs the collar of my t-shirt and pulls me closer.

My eyes close as I wrap my other arm around her and line our bodies up, turning her, so her back is to the wall. Her mouth opens and the tips of our tongues meet. We're about to cross the line beyond what happened out on the snow.

Our tongues circle each other, and her hands go into my hair, holding me close.

Her breasts are pressing into my chest. I can't help but move my hips against hers, showing her without words what she is doing to me. I'm not about to fuck her against the wall in the room where her cousin is getting married in a couple of days. No matter how much I want to.

It's hard to pull away. I forget everything else going on. All I care about is her mouth, her skin, the warmth of her body, and the passion in this kiss.

I move my hand from her waist, lifting the hem of her sweater until my fingers touch the warm skin of her stomach, just above her waistband. Her breath hitches, her abdomen constricts at my touch.

Eve's neck tilts as my mouth moves from her lips, down her throat and collar bone, then back up beneath her ear.

She smells and tastes amazing. My hips grind into her and she moans again. My erection presses between her thighs, she parts her legs to accommodate me.

When I pull back, she's panting as she stares at me. Her lips are red from the brutality of the kiss. We have to stop.

"Dash?"

My forehead drops to hers and I close my eyes.

"Come to my room."

My brow furrows. "I'm leaving in a couple of days, maybe even tomorrow."

"All the more reason to come to my room tonight."

"Are you sure?"

"I wouldn't have asked if I wasn't."

Her hand moves down between us, gliding over my belt and pressing against the front of my jeans. She cups me, taking my cock in her hand through my jeans.

Groaning, I drop my forehead to her shoulder as she continues to knead me, and my hips move.

"Fuck," I curse.

"That is the plan," she turns her head and her tongue trails over my pulse, soft open-mouthed kisses gently suck on my skin.

Before this goes too far, I step back and grab her hand. In silent agreement, we turn and hurry across the room.

Fortunately, we don't encounter anyone as we cross the lobby. The reception is quiet too. Guess there is no need for them to be on duty when everyone staying here is already checked in.

I figure the need might cool as we make our way up the stairs and along the corridor to her room. If anything, my erection is even harder, more painful within the confines of my jeans.

Eve fumbles her key, after a couple of tries, she finally gets the door open. We practically fall inside. I put a hand to the back of her neck and turn her, our lips finding one another again. The door slams a little harder than I intended when I kick it shut, reaching behind her to lock it.

"Are you really sure?" I ask her again.

"Shut up, Dash."

She grabs the bottom of my t-shirt and lifts it over my head. I take over and toss it on the floor as Eve dips her head. Her tongue flicks out against my nipple. Holy fuck. She peppers kisses across my chest as she undoes the button and zipper of my jeans.

Both my hands slam against the wall beside her head. Eve pushes my waistband down and wraps her fingers around the hard length of my cock. Her hand moves up and down a couple of times and I press my mouth to hers. There is nothing gentle about this kiss. I devour her and practically tear her sweater off, our lips only parting so I can remove the clothes from her body.

"Fuck," I ground out as her thumb strokes over the head of my cock.

I need to get my hands on her too. It's been too long, and the excitement rippling through my body is enough to make me pull back to stop her before I embarrass the shit out of myself.

Her hand falls between us and she looks up at me.

"These have got to go," I grab the waistline of her leggings and tug them. Making sure I get her panties at the same time because it's efficient.

Eve spreads her thighs and helps me, kicking off the leggings. Without pausing I press two fingers into her. She's so fucking wet for me. So ready. Using the other hand, I pull the straps of her bra from her shoulders, pushing one cup down so I can take her nipple into my mouth.

"Yes," she moans, gripping the back of my head and pulling me into her breast.

Curling my fingers upwards, I reach for that sensitive spot inside of her and she gasps, her head falling back as my thumb circles her clit. Eve writhes on my hand, growing wetter by the second.

Using one hand, I push my jeans down over my ass, freeing myself enough so I can run my length through her opening.

No matter how much I want to pick her up, wrap her legs around my hips and thrust into her, common sense takes hold. I thank the fucking stars above that I keep a condom in my wallet. It would have been a real fucking travesty to have to stop this.

I move her around and press her onto the bed as I take my pants off, and grab my wallet from my pocket. Eve watches me, her eyes hooded as she sits up and removes her bra, bearing her gorgeous tits to me. I tear open the condom, slide it on, then climb on top of her. It's on the tip of my tongue to ask her again but she spreads her legs wide and grips my waist.

No more questions are needed as I push my cock into her. Slowly, so slowly I ease inside, her head tips back. Running my tongue up her neck, I press all the way inside and hold still for a few moments. She shifts her hips, squeezing me until I can no longer stay still.

I begin thrusting, picking up the pace. Her body moves beneath me, her tits bouncing with every hard thrust. It takes every ounce of effort not to come right then and there at the sight of her.

Fuck, I don't want this to end too soon. Our lips meet again as I push my hand between our bodies and find her clit.

She cries into my mouth as I thrust inside, pressing her clit between my thumb and forefinger, teasing and flicking the small bundle of nerves.

Her breath comes faster, her moans take over, and she squeezes me tight. I grip the sheets by her head and hold on until she flutters around me. Eve comes so hard, her mouth falls open and her thighs lock around my hips.

Shit, I can't hold on, not when I see the complete ecstasy on her face as the orgasm rips through her. I thrust faster, pounding into her until I come too, releasing into the condom what feels like endlessly.

I'm panting hard, my heart pounding. I almost drop my body onto her, but prop myself up and lower my forehead between her breasts. Her chest is rising and falling, her breath coming in short, sharp bursts.

When I finally catch my own breath, I lift up and sit back on my knees, pulling off the condom and tying it. Eve's eyes remain closed, and she licks her lips. Jesus, I've never seen anything so fucking gorgeous in my life. She's perfect.

My eyes roam greedily over her body, her thighs still open and resting around my hips. I stroke my hand across her breastbone, tracing the slightly darker area of skin on the underside of her left breast.

It's a small birth mark that I long to trace with my tongue. But that seems strangely intimate. Which is a fucking insane thought after what we just did. Nothing could be more intimate than coming inside of her.

I flop down on the bed, resting one hand on my stomach, the other holds the condom away from her. The silence lengthens as I stare at the ceiling. It's not totally uncomfortable but I'm not sure what to say to her.

When I went downstairs, miserable as fuck, wanting to get away from everyone, I never thought I'd end up here. The sex was phenomenal. Kissing her is exquisite and addicting. So much so...

Rolling onto my side I take her cheek in my palm and turn her to face me. Her eyes are hooded, and her hair is a mess, but she's never looked more beautiful.

Eve melts into the kiss, one hand grasping my wrist. She drags it down her body, placing it over her breast. I almost grin but her tit feels amazing in my palm, her nipple hard and begging to be sucked.

So I do. She lets out another breathy moan as I circle the peak with my tongue. I might be getting on in years, but it isn't stopping my cock hardening again.

I only had one condom. Fucking idiot. I'm not ready for this to be over. I shift over her, getting between her thighs again and move down her body, kissing her as I go. My hand trails after my mouth, over the dampness on her skin.

Her head lifts and our eyes meet as I take the backs of her thighs and lift them over my shoulders. I've always enjoyed going down on a woman. Some guys don't and I've never understood that.

Eve cries out as I circle her clit with my tongue, then lower my face, nudging it with my nose as I lick a path up her opening.

When I dip inside, she makes the most insanely sexy breathless moan and grips the back of my hair, her hips thrusting up, wanting more. I keep going, adding two fingers, until she yells out, her body contracting. Opening my eyes, I watch as she plucks at her nipples, heightening her pleasure.

Why haven't we been doing this the whole time I was here?

Because Eve isn't that kind of woman. And I'm usually not the kind of man to jump into bed with a woman I've known for three days. It feels like I've known her a lot longer. I rest my head where her thigh meets her hip, not pressing down but relaxing.

Her fingers come down and play with my hair.

"I'm pretty sure I can break into my cousin's bedroom and steal her condom stash."

I chuckle and run a finger up her thigh, trailing it along the crease beside her pussy. Not going near her opening, even though her hips move at the contact. Lifting my head I look up at her and she smiles down at me.

"Are you suggesting we stay here and screw one another all night?"

"It wouldn't be the worst way to spend the evening," she muses.

I push myself up and over her. She glances between us, my cock is hanging heavy, touching her lower stomach. As much as I would love to take her up on that offer, I'm not sure it's the best idea. I kiss her abdomen then move to sit on the edge of the bed.

Eve sits up and puts her chin on my shoulder.

"You don't have to go. But I won't beg you to stay."

"It's not that I don't want to."

"What is stopping you?"

I turn my head as she lifts hers and we stare at each other. She's forthright, I'll give her that. Truth is, I don't have an answer for her.

Eve shifts beside me and gets off the bed. I watch her ass as she walks to the chair by the window and picks up a t-shirt. She slips it over her head. It trails to mid-thigh, the V-neck dips low.

How is it possible she looks even more sexy like this? The mounds of her breasts and the hard points of her nipples push against the fabric. My already half hard cock perks up again at the sight of her *covered* body.

As I watch her, she moves to the credenza where the complimentary drinks are and flicks on the tea kettle. I thought it was a bit kitsch having a kettle with tea and coffee making packets. A little touch of Europe in rural Wyoming.

"Do you want some tea?" she asks, her back still to me.

Do I? Her long, lean legs draw my eyes. I'm almost tempted to go over and push my hand under the hem, grab her ass and press my cock against it.

I surprise myself with my response. "Yeah, actually that would be nice."

I've never drank tea in my life. Guess I'm about to start.

My underwear and jeans are lying on the floor by the door. While she does whatever you need to do to make tea, I step into them and walk over to the seating area by the window.

Sitting down, I pull the curtains back to look outside. The snow has stopped again. If it stays off overnight, chances are the conditions will be a lot better. Which means I'll be able to leave. I frown at the table, not sure how I feel about it.

These last few days have been surreal, one surprise after another. Two disasters, a monumental disappointment and the best lay in recent history. All while surrounded by incredibly welcoming, funny and a great group of people. Especially the woman opposite me.

Eve sets a steaming mug in front of me and then sits down, drawing both legs up so her feet are beneath her butt.

"I made it how I like it," she says, indicating the drink.

It's a murky brown color, not quite as dark as coffee. She sets a packet of complimentary cookies on the table too.

"Thanks." I lift it and take a mouthful. It's hot as fuck and not totally unpleasant. Weird though, kind of tasteless. I'm not sure it's something I'll rush to try again. I wonder where she got the taste for tea but don't ask.

Eve smirks as she sips her drink. Her eyes lock on mine over the mug. She holds it in front of her face for a long moment.

"I'm starting to sound like a broken record, but will you leave tomorrow?"

"I'm not going to say yes or no because every time I think I can, something else comes up."

"Do you spend Christmas with your sister?"

"Yeah, and our dad."

She lifts a brow, and it's on the tip of her tongue to ask.

"Mom passed away three years ago. Breast cancer."

"Oh God, I'm sorry, Dash."

"Thanks. It's still weird without her. Time doesn't exactly heal all wounds, but it gets easier." I frown as I think about all the people who are here that I've met. "Is your dad..."

"Oh, very much alive. Yeah. My parents are going through a divorce. It hasn't been amicable at all," she lowers her mug and looks out of the window. "On mom's part mostly," she adds after a moment. "They won't tell us what happened, but I know it was something bad. And I know they don't have to give us all the details, but the speculation is driving me crazy."

"How long were they together?"

"Thirty-two years."

"Wow, long time."

"Yeah. I had no idea there were problems."

"Maybe they didn't want to upset you."

She shrugs. "Maybe. And I know I don't have the right to pry, but it's driving me crazy. They never showed us anything. Now it's like the worst thing ever has happened. Mom wouldn't let him come to the wedding, even though Ashlynn wanted him here."

My brows lift. "That's too bad."

She heaves out a breath and takes more tea. As if pushing it aside. There isn't a lot that could cause that much amount of animosity. Cheating? But which one. Statistically it is the husband. That doesn't mean women don't do it either.

I can imagine it is driving Eve crazy. "You'll still be here for Christmas?"

"Yep, Ashlynn has a whole thing planned. We were all told to bring one gift for Christmas morning. I'm heading back the day after though. I have a lot of work to get done around New Year."

If only I had that same problem. I shake the thought away. I've got work lined up. The company is going to live for at least another couple of months.

"Carter convinced Ashlynn to go somewhere warmer for their honeymoon."

My eyes go back to Eve. "I think he's probably had his fill of the snow for a lifetime."

She smirks and looks down at her drink.

I should go. Before I take her up on the offer to go raid someone else's stash of condoms. Talking about her family plans has brought it home more. I don't really belong here.

No matter how attracted I am to her, no matter how interesting I find her and would really like to spend more time getting to know her. In and out of bed.

This is temporary. Something I'll remember for a long time, granted. I've never been one for wishful thinking. Like why doesn't Eve live in Wyoming? Why didn't we meet under different circumstances, and had longer to get to know one another?

When I say I should go, she hides the disappointment, setting her mug down and rising when I do.

She stands by the end of the bed as I put on the rest of my clothes. I don't know if we'll get any time alone together again, or even if I will see her again after I walk out. Reality is knocking on the door, hard. I have to do whatever I can to get home.

Eve gives me a soft smile. Before I go to the door, I walk back to her. Her eyes widen slightly but they close as I cup her jaw and kiss her. She doesn't touch me back, but she kisses me, pouring a lot into the kiss that I choose not to read into.

I pull back and stare at her. Neither of us speaks. I don't want to say goodbye. I stroke my thumb over her bottom lip and then leave the room, closing the door carefully behind me. At least I don't have to go far.

As I turn, Holly is standing at the top of the stairs. She is staring at the door I just came out of. Shit. This is a problem I don't need to deal with. Giving her a quick chin dip, I enter my room and shut the door.

I might have just made Eve's day tomorrow a little more shitty.

Chapter 11

THE TOW TRUCK ARRIVES just after eight. I have the perfect view outside of my window, right above the inn's lobby. The windowsill is cold as I rest my ass on it, holding a hot cup of coffee, watching Dash as he talks to the driver. He's all wrapped up in his coat and a black hat that only makes him look even sexier than normal.

Together, the two men brush the snow off the truck, then Dash stands by and watches as he maneuvers the tow truck so he can hook it up, ready to be taken to God knows where. If Leon is right, the truck is going to the great big scrap heap in the sky.

I thought about going down to talk to him. To say goodbye to him but something about that final kiss makes me stay where I am. No words spoken, but said, nonetheless. I won't see him again.

God, I'm a fucking idiot. I've known him three days, had one great night with him. I should be happy I've broken the dry spell.

Spectacularly too. Dash knows how to fuck a woman that's for damn sure. My last two boyfriends never came close to how he made me feel. They certainly wouldn't have gone down on me after the deed. Rolling over and snoring was more likely.

I need to shower but like a crazy woman I like the smell of him on my skin. The sound of the tow truck rumbling to life draws my attention back outside. It moves slowly down the driveway, taking Dash's truck with it.

He stands alone in the drive, watching it go. A knock at the door breaks me out of my trance. A crazy notion of getting dressed and running down there took over my mind for a moment.

It's Ashlynn, and she's wearing a frown.

"What's wrong?" I ask.

"He's leaving?"

I roll my eyes and step back, letting her into the room. "Of course he's leaving. He doesn't live here. And he's not a guest at the wedding. He has a life to get back to."

My nonchalance sounds forced. Picking up my hat, I run it through my hands, keeping side-on to my cousin. Who knows me better than anyone. She looks at the bed as if she can see exactly what went on there last night.

Why do I feel so horrible? This is crazy. I go to the closet to get out my outfit for the day, all the while knowing Ashlynn is watching me.

"Honey?" she asks as I grab a pair of thick woolly socks out of a drawer.

"What?"

"Eve, look at me."

I raise my head. She tilts hers. "Fine, yes, we had sex. It was great. And now he's leaving, and that's that. There is nothing else to say about it."

She gives me sympathetic eyes. "Just great?"

I huff out a laugh. "Better than great. No matter what you think, Ash, this isn't what you hoped it would be."

"Did *you* hope it would be?"

"I'm a pragmatist. I live thousands of miles away from him. I don't know nearly enough about him to be sad about him... leaving." I rub my brow. "Shit, Ash. Why does this feel bad?"

"You know I believe in love at first sight," she shrugs.

"It's not *that.*" I brush off that idea quickly. "It's hard to explain. Maybe it's just because he's the first guy I've had any interest in for almost a year."

"Or maybe it's more than that but you're too scared to admit it."

"We can't all be as lucky as you finding our soulmate."

Ashlynn watches me for a moment. Whatever she sees makes a choice for her.

"I can see you don't want to talk about it, but I'm here when and if you do." Ashlynn comes over and rubs my back. "I'm getting married tomorrow," she says.

"Oh God, yes you are!"

Ashlynn's smile grows wider. "It's going to be really hard to avoid him today. He's under strict instructions not to come find me."

"You're really going with the whole not seeing each other the day before the wedding? Even now when we're all trapped here? How will you not run into him?"

"He's staying with his brother on the other side of the inn. And I told him he can't leave the room."

"Ash," I laugh.

She shrugs. "It's okay though because I have a lot to do and... I need my girls." She bites her lip, looking nervous all of a sudden.

"Come here," I pull her into a hug. She sniffles a little against my shoulder and I squeeze her tighter. "You're marrying the love of your life," I whisper.

"I know," she half laugh, half sobs. "It's a dream come true."

"You deserve it bitch," I say pulling back.

"So do you, jerk," she fires back.

"Well, I promise when you get back from your honeymoon you can help me find my own dream."

"You're on," she tugs on a piece of my hair, making me bat her hand away. "Now, I'm having breakfast brought up to my room.

Helene and Jessa are coming up too. We're having mimosas and are going to stay in our PJ's the whole day.

I grin at her, getting caught up in her excitement. In the back of my mind, I wonder if Dash is expecting to see me before he goes. The thought of that makes a lump form in my throat. It's best I don't see him.

Sex always complicates things. It was more than that, a voice whispers in my brain. I push it out.

I'm here for Ashlynn and I'm going to be present with her for the next two days. As much as Ashlynn can't wait for this, I can't wait to see it happen too.

Pretty soon, Dash Miller will be a distant memory.

We spend most of the day in Ashlynn's room, drinking champagne and playing the kind of games you would usually have at a bachelorette party. She takes a call from the wedding planner who says she is hopeful she'll make it up here tomorrow morning.

With the roads clearer it has made it easier to get here. She's become a good friend to Ashlynn, and she's ecstatic she is going to make it.

"We should go for a walk," Ashlynn announces. "It's stopped snowing and I want to build a snowman."

Helene laughs and sings the song from the Disney movie. She has a beautiful voice. We all agree we need air. We're all a little tipsy too from all the mimosas and champagne. I just hope none of us twist our ankles.

I head back to my room to change into something warmer and grab my things. Leon comes out of the room next door and says, hey. I smile but it doesn't reach my eyes. He's moved back in there. My heart sinks a little, but I push the thoughts away.

When I'm all wrapped up and ready to go outside, I come back out of the room and this time I run into Holly. She's glaring at me.

"Hey," I say as I shove my gloves into my pocket.

My first thought is to run past her and avoid talking but I've done that for most of the trip. She's spent a lot of time with mom and a couple of our cousins. I should make the effort. Stopping short of inviting her along, because Ashlynn wants this to be a bridal party thing. I wrack my brains for something to say.

"Morning. What do you think about you, me and mom grabbing dinner tonight?"

"I don't think so," she folds her arms over her chest.

"What's up, Holly?"

"As if you don't know."

"I'm drawing a blank," I shake my head.

"Dash."

"What about him?" My brows dip. Is he still here?

I've avoided going downstairs, and suspect it had a lot to do with why Ashlynn stayed up here too. Whether she admits it or not, she's got my back. She knows I don't want to discuss it, but can also see it's affecting me more than I want to let on. I don't understand it so there is no way I can articulate it to her. Or my sister.

"I saw him leaving your room last night. Really Eve. You barely know him."

Great. As if she wouldn't have done the same thing if Dash had shown even an inkling of interest in her. I feel bad for thinking that.

"Since when is what I do any of your business?"

"I'm your sister."

"When you feel like it."

"What is that supposed to mean?" she moves closer.

"I don't want to fight, Holly. There is enough bad blood between the people in our family. Just forget what you saw. It was no big deal."

She scoffs. I've got no idea why she is so angry. What does it matter to her what I did? Besides jealousy, which I kind of hope my sister would grow out of.

"We're not fighting," she snaps. "I'm just sick of being the one left to handle everything."

"What are you talking about?"

"You're never around."

"I'm busy with work. And I am around. When I'm not I call and speak to mom and dad all the time."

"Mom and dad, yeah," she rolls her eyes. "Not me though. I don't recall you even bothering to get in touch when I went through the divorce."

I did but... Not much. Where the hell is this coming from?

"You've hardly been around through this mess with mom and dad either. I'm the one who has dealt with everything."

"What do you mean by that?"

"If you were around, you'd know."

"You know why they split?"

She uncrosses her arms and looks to the left, to the door beyond Dash's. Is that mom's room? The room where Dash heard someone yelling on the phone?

Holly's expression changes and she lets out a shaky breath.

"She told me last night. And... I was coming to talk to you, because I needed my sister. Dash was coming out of your room."

My heart drops at the look on her face. This isn't really about Dash at all. Taking a step closer, I soften my voice. "We can talk now."

"I heard Ashlynn say the bridesmaids are going for a walk. Don't you need to go?"

Ashlynn will understand. She knows how contentious my relationship is with my sister. I still love her. Despite her faults, she is my sister. From the look on her face, she's hurting. I've wanted to know for months what happened between our parents.

I don't wish things were different last night. Being with Dash meant something but I also wish I'd been there for Holly.

"Let's go and get some hot chocolate. I can catch up with Ash and the girls."

"Why?" she asks, suspicious.

"We should talk. You look like you need it, Hol and I'll always be here for you."

She sniffs, not wanting to agree with that. But she nods. I ask her to give me a moment to let Ashlynn know, then we meet in the lobby. I watch my cousin and the others heading out, Ashlynn giving us a concerned look.

We grab our hot chocolate and go to the back of the inn, taking a seat close enough to feel the warmth from the fire but far enough away that the other people who've dared venture outside can't hear us.

I haven't seen mom at all today, which isn't surprising given I was sequestered upstairs. Come to think of it, I didn't see much of her yesterday either.

"What happened last night?" she asks me.

"I don't want to talk about that," I say, looking into my hot chocolate.

After a few moments of silence, I look up at my sister. Her eyes have softened more than I've seen in a long time. She could be a bitch and stick it to me about Dash, but she doesn't, and I appreciate that.

Finally she tells me what is wrong.

"Mom had a fight with dad last night."

"How?"

"He called saying he wanted to come up here, for the wedding. And to see us. It's Christmas Eve, eve," she adds.

I let out a sharp breath. God, how have I not realized what day it is?

One of our family traditions is to get together on the night before Christmas Eve. It is something dad always did with his family growing up and he kept up the tradition with us. It's nothing overtly special. We spend the day together, watch a Christmas movie, wear Christmas jumpers and take stupid pictures.

It breaks my heart a little to know dad wants to be with us today but can't. I hate the thought of him being alone. From the look on her face, Holly feels the same.

"What happened when he spoke to mom?"

"She was adamant he couldn't come. And, Eve, as much as I want him to come, knowing what I know now, I'm not sure he should."

My heart falls through the floor. I've suspected all along that there was someone else involved in this breakup. I never believed dad could do it. I can say the same thing about mom.

"About three months ago, mom had a health scare."

"What? What kind of health scare," I sit up straight, almost spilling my hot chocolate.

"She's fine. She thought she might have had cancer. She went through some tests."

"Oh God," I sit back and stare at the fire pit. It's a strange feeling to find out your mom may have had a life-threatening disease, but she doesn't, all within the span of three seconds.

"Why didn't she tell us?"

"She didn't want to worry us."

"Dad knew?"

"Of course. And he supported her through it. He wanted to tell us. She convinced him not to."

That must have killed dad. Beside Holly and my differences at times, we are all close.

"So, how did that turn into them getting divorced?"

"It made mom re-evaluate her life. Knowing she could have died."

"But she didn't and never would have," I shake my head. "If she wasn't actually sick."

Holly agrees with a look. She rubs her brow as if she doesn't want to say the next part.

"What happened?"

"She..."

"She had an affair?" My mouth drops open.

"Not quite... Well not conventionally."

Now I'm even more confused. "Just tell me Hol."

"She has worked with this guy for a few years, and said there was always an attraction there but she never acted on it because she loves dad. But after the scare, she started to think about what she might have missed out on. You know they've been together since high school. The only person they've been with is each other."

I always thought it was romantic. My parents were couple goals. Always so happy, which is what made the divorce even more of a shock.

"Mom made dad an indecent proposal, I guess. One night, with this guy. She said she wanted to live a different life for one night. That it would mean nothing, and they'd go on as normal once it was done."

"What the fuck," I breathe out.

"Yeah," Holly gives a sarcastic laugh.

"What did dad say?"

"No, of course. How was he supposed to accept that? For her to spend a night with this guy then go on as if nothing happened. As though it wouldn't break dad's heart."

Tears pool in my eyes for my father. This is worse than I ever could have imagined.

"Did she do it?"

Holly nods. "She told dad she was going out with work and that she would be staying in a hotel with him. When she came home the next day, she expected him to just... get over it."

"Fucking hell." I set the hot chocolate on the table beside me before I spill it.

"Mom thought I would side with her, that I'd understand. She figured I'd get pissed like she did that dad filed for divorce. He moved out and said he didn't want to talk to her for a while. Eve, she still can't comprehend what she did wrong."

"This is insane."

"Tell me about it. Listening to her trying to justify that she got a fucking *hall pass* last night was insane. She said he should just get over it," she repeats. "She even said she should be allowed to experience something different because if she died, she would have died not knowing what it was like to be with someone else. She blames dad for the divorce. Like she didn't cause it."

We sit in silence for a while, both lost in our thoughts. I can't believe our mother did that. Or that she thinks dad is to blame. My heart hurts. I want nothing more than to go to him. And tell mom to go to hell. How could she do something so fucking cruel?

No wonder he didn't want to tell us what happened. Or her. Although by the sounds of it, she feels no guilt whatsoever.

"I'm not sure I can face her," I say.

"That's exactly how I felt."

"What did you say to her after she told you?"

"I called her all the names under the sun. God Eve, I told her she was a bitch. That she didn't deserve dad. And she should spend the rest of her life miserable and alone. I didn't want to look at her."

Whoa, that was a lot. And then she came looking for me. She really needed me last night.

"What a fucking mess," is all I can think to say.

"That is an understatement. I know how it feels," Holly adds quietly. Her husband cheated on her a few times before their divorce. "It's not something you get over easily."

She looks at me with guilt in her own eyes. It wasn't the same thing, but Holly knows she tried to steal two of my boyfriends when we were younger. It's written all over her face how bad she feels about it.

"I wanted Dash."

My eyes rise to meet hers.

"Seeing how he looked at you pissed me off."

I keep my mouth shut. This wasn't where I thought she would take the conversation.

"Then he came out of your room and mom just told me all that crap and I felt like shit. I spent the whole night awake, pacing, thinking... Eve," she pauses, frowning into her drink. "I've been a bitch to you. Over the years."

"All sisters are like that."

"You preferred Ashlynn to me."

True. "We are closer in age. Hol, you had a different life to mine, you're older."

"Thanks for the reminder," she rolls her eyes.

"I just mean I had more in common with Ashlynn and, you had your own group of friends."

She nods and looks at the fields behind the inn. A faraway look enters her eyes that I can't read. The truth is, I don't know my sister as well as I know my cousin. After a moment she takes a deep breath.

"When I got up this morning, I called dad. I told him I know what mom did, and I was going to tell you too."

"What did he say?"

"He's sorry we had to find out about it. He wishes we didn't have to deal with the weight of mom's choices. Eve," she sniffs a few times. "I think he was crying."

I squeeze my eyes shut. I don't know how I am going to face our mother after this.

"It's breaking his heart to miss Ashlynn's wedding."

It's hard but I blink back the tears threatening to fall. They're borne out of anger and frustration more than anything else. "How did mom get him to stay home?"

"Dad doesn't want to cause trouble. The thing is, I could see the guilt in mom's eyes. She won't admit it, but she knows she's done him wrong. I think she's been hiding in her room."

"She better stay there, because I don't know what I will do if I see her," I snap.

"Same," Holly says. After a moment, she reaches between us and takes my hand.

I squeeze it back. Maybe I don't have much in common with my sister. I will find it hard to forgive the things she did when we were kids, but we at least agree on this. If we weren't here for Ashlynn's wedding, if it was just a family get together, we would have both been on the next flight home to dad.

"You should go catch up with Ashlynn. It's her wedding tomorrow. I'm sure she needs her maid of honor."

I don't particularly want to leave Holly alone. She gives my hand one last squeeze, then let's go. "I'm going to call dad again."

"I will too," I say. "I want him to know I wish he was here. He deserves to be here more than mom."

"This is so messed up."

We're in complete agreement there. Dad coming up here is a bad idea. I want him to know that I love him, miss him and will be on his side through this. I'm not sure how I can ever face mom again.

Taking my leave of Holly I walk down the back steps onto the field. I don't know where my cousin and the others will be and that is okay, because I just want to be alone right now.

I text Ashlynn to let her know my talk with Holly is taking longer than I planned and she sends me one back telling me to take my time.

I walk for a while, up the slopes where the sledding competition was held, over to where there is a long line of trees, separating the inn's property line from whatever lays beyond.

The sky is blue and cloudless. It's on course to be the perfect conditions for the wedding tomorrow, provided the snow stays off. It's absolutely pristine out here. My footprints are the only ones leading across this field.

I want to call dad. What do I even say to him? The divorce was bad enough, knowing why it's happening is soul destroying.

Using my gloved hand, I brush away the tears that have fallen and try to blink the rest of them away. Ashlynn doesn't need to know about this, not till after the wedding, after her honeymoon. I want people to know dad isn't the villain, but he'll want to keep this quiet.

That's the kind of man he is. I sniff again and turn around to head back and find Ashlynn. I almost scream when I see a man standing a few feet away. I hadn't heard a thing.

"Dash?" I blurt out in shock.

What the hell is he still doing here?

Chapter 12

The cold was seeping into my ass where I was sitting on a random bench at the back of the inn. I wanted to get away from all the people. Not that I don't like being around them, but I need time to think.

My truck has been towed away. The guy gave me his card and said he'd call to let me know if the truck is salvageable. He seemed optimistic, but he hasn't been under the hood yet. It is the end of an era. I've been through a lot in that truck.

It holds a huge number of memories. Some good, some bad. Some sexy ones, when I was younger. I almost lost my virginity in there three times, just never managed to take that final step for one reason or another. At least two of them were with the same girl.

The plan is to get out of here as soon as possible. I've imposed enough and my family are back home waiting for me. It is the right time to go.

Part of me is sad to go, these people are great and if we lived closer, we might have become friends. Which makes me think about the other person I might have had more with.

'What ifs' are pointless dwelling on. It is what it is.

Last night happened for a reason and it ended the way it was supposed to. With me driving out of here without causing any more drama for the family.

And then the fucking rental company called to say the car they were expecting back hadn't made it. In fact, it had been totaled by the idiots driving it into a ditch and hitting a tree. I mean, I felt for them and did ask if they were okay, but it didn't help me in that moment.

I'd called around a couple of other places, but no one could help. I'd contemplated calling an Uber but that wouldn't work. I'd have to re-mortgage my house to pay for it.

What I could do was get a room at a hotel in Evergreen Hollow. And that was the plan until Chase found me calling around the hotels up there. Chase is what I would consider the human version of a golden retriever. He hounded me until I told him the situation. He laughed, grabbed me by the shoulder and said there was no way they would let me leave.

Whose fucking room I was going to end up in next is beyond me. I tried to talk him out of it but the more people he told, they all pressured me to stay. And not just for the night. Stay for the wedding. Chase called me the 'mascot', which was pretty fucking insulting. The guy is so infectiously charming, I couldn't give him shit about it.

He brought out the big guns, getting Carter to come talk to me.

I politely declined, and he managed to call Chase off. I don't particularly want to stay in Evergreen Hollow. It will mean driving past the plot of land where the hotel I *wouldn't* be building is.

So I look at towns in the same direction as home. A motel on the highway said they have rooms but check-in isn't until after three, which is four hours away. Now all I need is a cab. I can find a coffee shop to hang out in. Or a bar.

The guys are trying to keep Carter away from Ashlynn. Because of course she is a stickler for tradition. And now that they have a way to get off the inn's property, they got cabs to take them into town and the local bar there. I, of course, got roped in.

Now I'm back and a little worse for wear, those firefighters sure can drink. A few of them talked about Eve and me, giving me shit about her but I said nothing was going on.

Carter eyed me the whole time. I don't know if Eve told Ashlynn, she probably did. Women do stuff like that. And she will have told Carter. He changed the subject, sensing my discomfort.

It's not like I think of her as a one-night stand. It meant a lot more than that but looking at it rationally, that's what it was.

I'm beginning to feel like I'm never going to get out of Noel Ridge, especially the Ridgewood Inn. Something keeps bringing me back here.

I don't deliberately set out to avoid Eve. The walk across the surrounding land will clear my head. Give me the chance to get my thoughts straight about the lost opportunity and how I'm going to tell Daria.

Which I still haven't done.

Seeing Eve by the trees, looking out over the snowy fields hit me like a fucking sledgehammer. No matter what I do, I run into her. I don't turn back as if I haven't seen her. I want to go to her. I'm not sure how to process that.

When she turns, there are tears on her cheeks. Jesus fuck. Did I do that?

No, that doesn't fit with who she is. She wouldn't be crying over me. Which begs the question, what the fuck is making her cry?

"I thought you left," she says across the snowy land between us.

"Can't seem to get away from this place," I answer, taking a few steps closer.

Any normal guy would run a mile but Eve matters to me. Seeing her cry does something to me. There is a deep-seated need to fix it. To take away whatever pain is causing her tears. Even if it's me.

"Are you alright?" I ask. Okay, so I'm hoping against hope she doesn't say this is because of me, that small niggle of doubt remains.

"Yeah. Well," she frowns and looks away, wringing her gloved fingers together. "I found out this morning what happened with my parents."

Oh. Okay, good. Well, shit not *good*. But... I push away my own fears about her tears and walk to her.

My sister used to cry a lot when she was a teenager. My go to was to make fun of her. She's my sister and it was usually over something stupid so I could get away with it.

I never felt like this when I saw Daria cry. Or any other woman for that matter. Eve doesn't let any more tears fall. She pulls herself together better than most.

"Do you want to talk about it?" I ask, stopping in front of her.

"Why aren't you halfway to Cheyenne?"

"You want me to go?" I arch a brow.

"No. I'm just surprised you're still here."

You and me both. I don't bother filling her in on where I've been the past couple of hours. While she thought I was driving home, I was in the local pub with her family and friends.

"The plan is to head to a motel about ten miles or so from here later on."

"A motel. Nice."

"It's ten miles closer to home. So, how did you find out about your parents?"

She heaves out a very heavy sigh. "Do you mind if we walk and talk? I think if I stand still, I might lose my shit and you don't want to see that."

"Probably not."

We start walking. For the first few minutes, in silence. It is like she's building herself up to tell me and I can't help wondering what the fuck happened with her parents. It's definitely not what I thought she was going to say.

I'm pretty pissed for her, for her dad, even Holly. But mostly, I'm pissed about my own mom. She didn't survive her cancer diagnosis. She suffered and eventually succumbed to her illness and my dad stood by her through it all.

This is... for want of a better word, diabolical. Who does something like that? It's blown up her whole family. My jaw is tense as we stop by a wooden fence.

Across the open land you can just about make out another property. They probably have horses that would be out in the open pasture in better weather. We've walked a long damn way. Eve leans against one of the heavy fence posts and stares into the distance.

"I'm so torn over what to do," she says.

"In what way?"

"I want dad here, but I don't want him to have to deal with mom. I don't want him to be alone for Christmas, but I can't abandon Ashlynn."

"Tough spot," I lean my elbows on the next fence post over.

"You know we have this tradition in our family. Most people have family gatherings on Christmas Eve, so that they can spend Christmas Day with their immediate family. Not us."

"No?" I turn to face her. She's right, that is the way things happen in our family. Except while I'm single, Daria drags my ass to her place on Christmas Day. Not that I'm complaining. I still spend most of it alone, usually chilling watching movies and drinking beer, until it's time to go around for dinner.

"We have a Christmas Eve, eve day."

Ah. "So that would be today?"

She nods. "It's the one day of the year when we make the effort to be together. No matter what is going on. My whole life we've never missed one. Now dad is alone and... hurting. Is it wrong to want to smash your mom's teeth out?"

"Usually I'd say yeah," I say with a wry smile. "It's never right to hit a woman, especially your mom."

"I guess," she rolls her eyes. After a moment she smiles. "Dad used to tell me Christmas Eve, eve was my day. When I was a kid, I believed him because of my name."

"I got that," I laugh.

"He said it was our secret though because he didn't want to upset Holly. He never played favorites, he loves us equally but dad and I were closer. We share a lot of the same interests. I'm less dramatic than Holly," she adds with a laugh.

"How'd she take the news?"

"About as well as I did. She hasn't spoken to mom since and she doesn't want to. I think she wants dad to come up here."

"I'm not sure that's a good idea," I say. "If you want my opinion, that is."

"You're right, don't worry," she gathers some snow from the fence and starts to shape it into a snowball. "I can't stop thinking about him being alone."

"He has friends, other family he can go to?" I ask.

"Yeah, and he'll be with them for the next few days. With people who care about him. It's just..." she tosses the snowball. "Not us."

Her lips twist as she looks around, then she focuses on me. "Oh shit, your ankle. We've been walking for ages."

"It's fine," I wave her off. "It wasn't as bad as everyone thought."

"My socks are wet."

I can't help but laugh at the sudden change of topic. "Mine too."

"We should go back."

"Yeah, my balls are freezing off."

"Well, we can't have that," she grins. "That would be a travesty."

We trudge back through our own footprints. Our shoulders brushing every now and then. I don't know what it is that keeps drawing us back together. I'm not sure I want to question it. As the inn comes into sight, our pace slows a little.

Eve pauses and I take a few more steps before I realize. I turn to face her. Her smile is mischievous as fuck.

"One more for old times' sake."

My mind automatically goes to how uncomfortable it will be fucking her in the snow. I've tried sex on the beach and the sand got in all the wrong places. Snow presents a whole host of other problems. Her brow arches as she sees me calculating all this.

"I meant a snowball fight, perv."

"What? I knew that." I laugh.

"Sure you did."

"You don't know what you're letting yourself in for," I put my hands on my hips and stare her down.

"I thought that last night, but I coped okay."

More than okay. Jesus, this woman. She drops to her knees and starts frantically making a snowball. Shit. I do the same and before I've even formed one, a mushy half falling apart snowball smacks into my face. I yell out and launch my own wildly.

Unfortunately, it misses. Not only that, but I'm such an expert it didn't break apart, so she launches mine back at me and it hits me in the forehead. I fall back in the snow, brushing it out of my face just as Eve looms over me. She's holding more snow. She hasn't even attempted to turn it into a ball.

I lift my arms to protect myself. "No!"

She drops the snow, and it covers my face, neck and chest. Eve laughs hysterically and tries to get away. Rolling over, I swipe at her legs, making her fall flat on her face. She screams and I move quickly, crawling over her. Not enough to crush her but enough that she can't get up and fight back.

"You're a cheat," I say into her ear.

"It's every man for himself in snowball wars, remember?"

"That wasn't even a snowball," I argue.

She bucks up and I ease back, letting her roll over but I don't move away. My mind goes back to that first kiss in the snow. It feels like it happened ages ago, but it was just a couple of days. And we've done far more than that since.

"It was a very short-lived snowball fight," she says, breathing a little harder than before.

The urge to kiss her is so strong, I have to physically force myself to lean back.

Is that disappointment I see in her eyes? We can't go there again. I'm leaving in... I look at my watch. An hour. Shit.

"I need to get back," I say, getting to my feet. I reach down and take both of her hands, pulling her up. We're chest to chest now.

"Let's go then," she takes a step back. "And we will never speak of the absolutely pathetic snowball fight again."

"Agreed."

We walk along in companionable silence. I'm glad I've taken away some of the sadness in her eyes when I found her out here. It'll be back. She's worried about her dad, and rightly so.

As we approach the front of the inn, a pristine black sports car is parked at the front. We glance at each other and Eve whistles.

"Is that a Maserati?" she asks.

"Looks like. What is it doing *here*? And how the hell did the driver get it here in these conditions?"

"You're so practical," she nudges me.

"It pays to be careful. Especially where the snow is concerned."

"Who do you think it belongs to? Maybe the firefighters got it for Carter, for a surprise ride or something?"

We walk down the slope onto the path around the inn, towards the car. A couple of the firefighters and some of Eve's younger male cousins are all cooing over the car. I can't help but stop and look at the beauty of the thing. It's got to be worth a few hundred grand.

"Dash."

I turn around at the voice calling my name. My mouth drops open when I see Lewis Henrickson standing on the porch of the Ridgewood Inn. I exchange a glance with Eve, who recognizes him from his picture on the website.

She grabs my arm. "Dash," she whispers.

I'm not getting my hopes up. Fuck. Why is he here though?

"Go talk to him," she gives me a gentle shove.

"Uh..."

Eve snort laughs. Lewis comes down the steps towards us and I feel like an ass for making him come to me. But, then again, why should I go running to him? Fucking hell, I'm starting to sweat.

"You got here just in time," he says, reaching for my hand.

"I did?" I shake his. He's wearing designer thick black gloves, with a fleece lined leather jacket, which looks as if it cost a whole month's paycheck.

"Yeah, I have a flight to catch and I'm gonna be late. If I hadn't been held up a few days cos of the weather, I wouldn't even have to fly." He shakes his head as if it really bothers him he has to take an airplane.

Lewis turns his gaze to Eve. He gives her an appreciative look over and I'm reminded of how good looking he is, and how he could very easily get any woman he wants. I take a slight step closer to her.

"I'm Eve," she says, sticking out her hand.

Lewis gives her a panty melting grin and introduces himself. He takes one look at me and his eyes widen a little before he releases Eve's hand. His look tells me he received the message. Not that I have any right to stand in the way. Maybe Eve wants to...

"I'll leave you two to talk," she says. Our eyes lock and she bites her lip, giving me a small nod.

The firefighters have gotten over their fascination with the car and follow Eve inside. There are a couple of inn staff shoveling snow again but they're not near us.

"You should have called," I say.

"I intended to, but I was passing on the way to the airport, and remembered you saying you were staying here because of the bad weather."

In all honesty, I don't remember telling him that. I must have done. Sweat trickles down my back. I can't get my hopes up and have them shattered again. It's hard not to when he is standing here in front of me.

"Look, I feel really bad about the whole thing with the hotel. Dad went with the other company. I couldn't convince them otherwise."

Yep, there is that hope being crushed beneath my soaked boots and uncomfortably damp socks.

"Then why are you here?"

"Because I have a proposition for you," Lewis says. His phone dings and he takes it out and looks at it, frowns and shoves it into his pocket. "I don't have a lot of time. I really liked your ideas for the hotel. I've researched you, spoke to a few people you've worked with."

My frown deepens. Not sure what I think about him checking me out. It can only be a good thing, right?

"Look, I'm breaking away from my dad because he's not open to change. And I get it, he's a different generation. You and I both know where the future lies, and I want to have my name associated with that. Not just because it's fashionable, because it's the right thing to do.

"I'm branching out with a smaller side to the company. It will be nothing on the scale of what we're currently working on. As far as I'm concerned that's more important than a hotel the mayor of a town wants built to draw tourists."

My head is nodding along with him. He's talking my language.

"In the next few weeks, I'm going to start looking at land I can acquire and want to start building some sustainable houses in low-income areas. I'm going to need someone with your expertise that I can trust to bring my plans to life."

"You're kidding?" the words fall out of my mouth, and I want to take them back because I sound like a fucking moron.

Lewis laughs. "Nope. Listen. I'm gonna be away till after New Year but I want to meet when I get back. I'll have my personal assistant call you." He steps over and slaps his hand onto my shoulder. "I think this is going to be the start of an amazing journey, Dash. Father's loss is my gain."

"That would be... great."

"Good. It's gonna take a while to get all my ducks in a row, so don't go turning down any work, but I want you to free up your calendar from around February onwards. The plan is to start then and once it gets going, I'm fully expecting it to snowball," he looks around with a laugh. "Pardon the pun. Right, I really gotta go. This is gonna be something special, Dash. I'm sorry I can't stop longer, thank Ashlynn and Carter for me."

Why am I not surprised Ashlynn and Carter have made an impression on him in a mere few minutes?

"Raine, my assistant will call you on January third. I'm excited about this. It's gonna be great."

I stand on the same spot as Lewis gets in the Maserati and turns in the driveway. The engine is so quiet, it's an electric car. Damn, he really is serious about taking care of the planet.

"What did he say?"

I turn to face Eve. I'm still in shock if I'm being honest.

"I think he just hired me to be his construction guy."

"On the hotel?"

"No," I shake my head. "On... Everything else."

"What? Dash, that's amazing," she grabs my sleeve. "See, I told you. If you are yourself, people are going to want to be a part of what you're doing."

"I'm still having a hard time believing this is real."

Tugging off my hat, I run a hand through my hair, bewildered by what just happened. Nothing is set in stone. He's not going to be ready till February and a lot can happen between now and then. But... This is fucking huge. This is beyond my wildest dreams. I can't get my head around it.

"Do you really think Lewis Henrickson would drive all the way to this inn, in the middle of a freakish snowstorm, just to give you lip service. Dash, he meant everything he said. He loved your designs, and he wants to work with you."

"Shit," I say. "Shit, I repeat.

Eve laughs and grabs my arm, shaking me out of the stupor I am currently in.

"I'm so happy for you," she throws her arms around my neck, and I wrap mine around her waist, half lifting her. "We need to celebrate," she pulls back. "Oh, you need to leave," the joy seeps out of her expression and she drops down off the balls of her feet.

"I can stay for a drink," I say, against my better judgement. "To celebrate," I add.

The motel will still be there in another hour. Even though it's starting to get dark, and I should be heading out. Definitely not standing here holding this woman in my arms.

One that is starting to mean a hell of a lot to me. It doesn't matter I've only known her a few days. She's made an impression. And she is going to be hard to get over.

Eve beams a smile. I'm still holding her in my arms. In all honesty, I don't want to let go. In fact, I want to kiss her. Her cheeks are rosy and her eyes bright, she's happy for me. Excited that Henrickson came here to tell me he wants me to work for him. Staring at her is fucking intoxicating.

I start to lean in, as she rises on her toes towards me.

Just as all the lights in the inn blink out.

Chapter 13

"Don't worry everyone, we're fully equipped for situations just like this," the Inn owner says.

He's not been around much, letting the manager and the other staff take care of everything. This is a bit of a catastrophe, so they've brought in the big guns.

He introduced himself as Alistair Ridgewood, telling us the inn has been in his family for over five decades. Standing just over six foot, his silver hair is combed back neatly, and he has a salt and pepper bushy mustache. His voice is warm and comforting, and I feel as if every word out of his mouth is trustworthy.

He's wearing a thick wool sweater over a checkered blue and yellow shirt, which is buttoned all the way up to his throat and a little bow tie sits neatly between the shirt and sweater. He's paired it with jeans and snow boots. He's a walking juxtaposition and I like him the minute I see him.

He doesn't rush as he talks, he's polite and listens intently when someone asks him a question.

Most of my family have gathered in the lobby, some are in the bar listening through the arch, enjoying a drink with their black out.

It wasn't so bad when the lights first went out because there was still daylight.

It's twilight now and the only light in the inn is from the fire and candles that have been placed around by staff. I shouldn't have been surprised to see them coming out of their office, setting out old glass and metal lanterns with large candles inside. They cast a lot of light around them. It was no wonder they were popular. Back in Victorian times.

The biggest problem with the black out right now, is the heat has gone off too, not just the lights.

"We're hoping that the grid will be back up and working before the night is through."

"The grid?" George asks.

"Yes, unfortunately, it's hit the whole town of Noel Ridge and some of the surrounding areas. I've been in communication with some colleagues and friends on my CB radio."

Dash snort laughs beside me. "Of course he has a CB radio."

"Hush," I nudge him.

He's stuck around, which I'm not going to complain about. I haven't asked him why. It might make him remember he was set to leave.

"We should be grateful of that radio right now," I say, pulling my coat around me. We're at the back of the lobby, close to the door and furthest from the fire.

"What caused this?" Carter's dad asks.

He's taken on the role of leader of the group which surprised me. He's mostly been quiet up to now. Once Mr. Ridgewood arrived, he took him to one side, and they talked for a moment before Mr. Ridgewood went to speak the staff. Since then, they started rallying to make the inn safe.

"Another storm front unfortunately. We've had an unprecedented amount of snowfall this year," he chuckles a little.

"Does that mean we're going to get *more* snow?" Carter's mom asks, clutching at her pearls.

"The forecast has taken everyone by surprise."

He laughs in response, which Carter's mom does not appreciate. In fact, she outwardly groans and scowls at no one in particular, or everyone in the room, depending on how you want to take it.

"The weather front was heading away but took a turn. It makes for a great white Christmas, not so much for a modern day stay at the inn. I want to reassure you all that we are in the process of starting up our generator. There will be electricity in the most needed places, such as the kitchen and communal areas.

"We would ask that you refrain from using your electronic devices via the sockets, charging and what not, as this will drain the generator. The staff will be providing more blankets for every room, and those where there are fireplaces, we can assist with getting them lit for you. We have plenty of lanterns.

"Would you please make sure that you keep the candles inside the lanterns once they are lit. I know it's cold," he quips. "But I'd rather we didn't start any fires."

There is a smattering of laughter. Most of it from the firefighters.

I find Ashlynn amongst all the other faces. So much for avoiding Carter today, they're standing side by side. Carter has his arm around her shoulder and she's leaning into him. Any other bride would be about losing their shit right now. Not Ashlynn.

She's fucking grinning like this is the best thing that ever happened. The woman is off her head.

"There will be plenty of hot drinks and a hot meal this evening. Then until the power is restored, the food will be cold but delicious. We have plenty to go around and the generators will keep the refrigerators running for a good sixteen hours. Things should be back up and running before then.

"If there are no further questions, we'll get on with making your stay as comfortable as possible."

A few people ask questions, but most people head off. Some of them help take blankets upstairs and the firefighters are busy passing out lanterns, saying they'll get them all set and lit for everyone.

Dash blows out a long breath and shakes his head.

"What's wrong?"

"I'm not getting out of here today."

"Why?"

"It's not safe on the roads. Have you ever driven in a black out?"

"No."

"It's impossible to see anything around you. Even with your headlights, and especially in this weather. It's too dangerous."

"That's... A shame," I twist my lips to stop my smile. "Whose room *will* you stay in next?"

"Yours of course," Ashlynn pops up next to us.

"God!" I almost jump out of my skin and push her away.

"Come on, we're all grown ups here, right Dash," she nudges him. He smirks at her and then looks at me with one brow raised.

I mean, I wouldn't leave him without anywhere to sleep. *Sleep*. Obviously.

"You can't catch a break," Carter says as he comes to stand with us. "If that guy hadn't held you up you could have been on the road before the power went out."

"The lights would have gone out while he was driving. Do you think he is okay?" Ashlynn's eyes widen.

"He'll be fine babe. It was still light when he set off. Besides, he looked like the kind of guy that only needs to make one phone call and an army will come running."

"He *is* loaded," I agree.

Carter doesn't comment. Even though his family is loaded too, he never talks about it, or spends it. He's happy living a normal lifestyle with Ashlynn. Sure, they can afford some of the finer things in life, but he never flaunts it.

"Looks like you're coming to the wedding," Carter gives Dash a pitying look.

"Everything should be fixed in the morning," he says. "The cab will be fine driving during the day."

"Dash, you'll still be here you might as well stay for the ceremony," Ashlynn interrupts. "We'd love to have you."

He looks like a deer in the headlights.

"Oh God, how romantic will it be if we move the wedding start time back a little," Ashlynn smiles.

"You want to delay marrying me, babe?"

"Of course not, but it will be gorgeous with all these lanterns."

"If that is what you want."

"It would make things so much more atmospheric and Christmassy," she smiles.

Dash's head is turning back and forth as they talk. He looks as if they're speaking a foreign language. I'm used to the way these two talk to each other. I can understand how your average person would find it all a little... sickening.

"And you my new friend, are staying. No arguments," Ashlynn tells Dash. "Now get out of my sight," she says to Carter. "I'm not supposed to see you before the wedding. It's bad luck."

"Not sure our luck could get any worse," I mutter.

"Now, now my pessimistic friend," Ashlynn hugs me to her side. "When the world gives you lemons."

"Make Lemon Drops," Helene calls as she breezes past. "I need alcohol stat."

Ashlynn and Carter kiss each other goodbye. He goes to the stairs to help with operation keep everyone comfortable at the inn. Ashlynn follows Helene. She winks at me as she passes.

"You don't have to stay," I turn to Dash.

"At this point, I'd feel like I'd let everyone down, and be the asshole if I left," he says with a sardonic eye roll.

"You're probably right."

"I don't need to stay in your room."

"Shut up, Dash."

"You say that a lot."

"You say things that make me have to say it."

"Like what?"

"Well, both times have been about coming to my room," I say in a low voice.

"This is different."

"Is it, really though?"

"Things are different, between us."

"What is your point?"

"I'm trying to be a gentleman."

"Why start now?" I say saucily over my shoulder. As I walk away, Dash smothers a smile. He stands in the lobby as I make my way over to the bar.

When he takes the stool beside me, I can't help but smile.

I'm not one to believe in fate, but the universe does seem to be stopping Dash from leaving.

Holly and I sit in a quiet corner of the dining room and call dad. He is worried when we tell him what happened with the power, but we reassure him the inn staff have everything covered.

By mutual decision we agree not to bring up the situation with mom, even though dad is aware we know what happened.

He's at his sister's house and they all gather around to say hi at the start of the call. No one asks where mom is. I don't know how much dad has told them, probably nothing.

Dad is in his late fifties, but he looks younger. I've always thought he's a handsome man, with more pepper than salt in his hair. He's fit, goes running every morning and has a great job.

He's been an amazing father and, from what I've witnessed, an amazing husband. Staring at him now, my heart silently breaks as I paste on a smile.

"You girls got your gifts ready, we all gotta open them together."

"Dad, we haven't been girls for at least a decade," Holly rolls her eyes.

"Speak for yourself," I say, giving dad a wink.

"No fighting, it's Christmas Eve, eve."

Holly and I take our gifts out of the bag dad gave her to bring here. On screen he pulls out two presents. Ours are similar in size. Dad has one large and one small. The small one is from me.

"Wait, wait," Dad gets up and disappears from the screen. He's back only a moment later, and he grins as *Merry Xmas Everybody*, by Slade starts playing.

"Oh, not that God awful song," Holly covers her ears. "I thought we were going to get away with it this year."

"Never Holly-bob," dad says, using her old nickname. "I want to hear you sing loud and proud at the chorus."

"Never happening," she picks up her gift as dad starts singing. Off key as usual.

A few people turn around and Ashlynn's dad cheers, knowing exactly what we're doing in the corner, but he keeps his distance, being respectful.

Dash looks over too and I give him a small smile. God what he must think about all this madness going on around him.

When we open our presents, we're both thrilled. Dad got us each a bracelet with a thin silver bar engraved with our names and 'love you always, dad'

Okay, now I'm crying. We help each other put them on and show him. He's smiling but everyone knows as clear as fucking day how devastated he is. But he puts on a brave face as he opens our gifts.

Holly's is a wooden foot massager. It looks like medieval torture to me, but dad loves it, saying his feet have been hurting after running and that will help a lot. Holly gives him a huge smile, but her hand reaches out towards me.

It feels strange to be comforting my big sister, especially given our relationship history but I hold on as dad unwraps my gift. He stares at the box, then grabs his glasses and reads the instructions.

"What did you get him?" Holly asks.

Dad starts laughing. "Oh, I gotta try this," he opens the package and takes out the stand. I already put batteries in for him. After some messing around, and getting our teenage cousin to come help, he finally gets it set up.

"What is it?" Holly asks again.

Dad laughs. "This is brilliant, where did you find this? Marty, look at this."

His brother comes over and leans down. Then he looks at the gadget. You set your phone into it, and it projects the image onto a 12-inch screen just in front of the phone stand. Because dad is always losing his glasses, or complaining the damn screen on his phone is too small.

"I love it, I love them both. And I love you both."

"Love you too dad," we say in unison, and he laughs again.

"Okay, enough of this, go get my niece. I want to have a chat with her before she marries that boy."

Holly blows dad a kiss and gets up to go get Ashlynn.

"You doing okay Evie-girl?" dad asks me.

"Just wish you were here," I say.

"I'll see you in a few days. Got a big party planned."

"I'll be there."

"Been pretty eventful up there, huh?"

"You wouldn't believe it dad. It's like Ashlynn is living her own Hallmark movie, mixed in with a little of the Marx Brothers."

"You're safe though, with the power out."

"Oh yeah, the inn has been amazing about everything."

"Good," he smiles at me.

I'm struck by that smile. It's something that has always been there, even during the hard times, dad always had a smile. He's doing it again.

Holly and Ashlynn appear and my crazy cousin sits on my lap, greeting dad with kisses that she blows at the screen.

"My three favorite girls," he grins. "I hope you are all looking after each other. And just because we're not together today isn't something to get upset about okay? We still have a lot of Christmas Eve, eve's in us."

We chat a little longer. Until dad asks for a moment alone with the bride. We wish him goodnight and say we'll speak tomorrow.

"Where is mom?" I ask Holly stiffly as we walk back to the bar.

"In her room, I think."

"Have you spoken to her?"

She shakes her head and lifts a brow. I shake back.

"Is it wrong that I feel bad?" I ask.

"No. What is wrong is that we've been put in this position by her actions."

Holly's words take me by surprise. They're very true. She's not usually someone to be so eloquent and to the point though.

"We'll forgive her, eventually, because she's our mom," Holly says. "It might take a while, but she isn't a bad person, she just made a very bad choice."

I'm not sure I'll be forgiving her any time soon, but I can appreciate Holly's words. She twiddles with the bracelet on her arm, then leans in and kisses my cheek.

"Have a good night." Her eyes flick to Dash at the bar and back to me. "Don't do anything I wouldn't do."

"That doesn't leave me with a lot of options."

"Rude," she pushes me, and I shove her back. She laughs, then heads towards the stairs.

Every second step has a small storm lamp on it to light the way. Ashlynn is right, the way the inn has been lit up is almost magical.

"You okay babe?" Ashlynn hugs me from behind.

"Yeah. How was your chat?"

"He said he'd come rescue me right now if I wanted out of this wedding." I roll my eyes. "He would always have our backs. That's what I love so much about Uncle Jack. I really wish him and your mom could work things out."

"Yeah."

That isn't happening. Ever. And if dad ever considered it, I'd do my best to talk him out of it. I'll never forgive mom for this. I turn to face her.

"Well, it's time to turn that frown upside down missy," she tickles me, making me squeal. "And have a good time tonight. But not too late, because I'm getting married tomorrow and I need you by my side," she grips my hands. "We start getting ready at nine."

"I'll be there. And I'll have the others with me. Don't worry. It's all going to be amazing."

She hugs me again and I watch her walk up the stairs. She does a little dance and spin at the top, then waves at me.

I slide back onto the seat beside Dash.

"How'd it go?" he asks. Besides Holly, he is the only person who knows the truth.

"Good, he seems happy at my aunt's house." I toy with the bracelet. Dash looks down so I hold it up to show him the inscription.

"It's beautiful," he says.

He must sense I'm not in the mood to talk because he signals the bartender and gets me a small glass of wine and himself a shot of whiskey. We drink in silence and watch the surrounding people. No one is letting the black out get to them.

God, I love my family.

Why did mom have to go and ruin everything?

I'm brought out of my melancholy when I realize Dash is standing up beside me. I look up at him, wondering when he did that. He holds his hand out to me. I don't say anything as I slowly slip my hand into his.

Dash gently pulls me up. Without saying a single word, we walk out of the bar and head upstairs to my room.

Chapter 14

Out of force of habit, when we enter the room, Eve flicks the light switch. Nothing happens, and she laughs at herself with a shake of her head. A warm glow is coming from inside. One of the giant lamps has been placed on the desk by the window, burning brightly enough that we can see where we're going.

Eve isn't lucky enough to have a fireplace in her room, so it's chilly when we go in. She shudders and crosses to the bed as I close and lock the door.

This is probably one of the surrealist moments of my life. I'm about to share a bed with this woman, who I'm insanely attracted to, have already had sex with, and gotten on well with. Yet I'm nervous.

What the fuck? I don't get nervous around women.

"Did you tell Daria about the offer?"

Eve's words snap me out of my thoughts. She has a box of matches and is lighting the Christmas candle. She's carried it to the bedside table so there is more light on the other side of the room to the lamp.

"Not yet. I wanted to tell her in person, then my cell phone died, and I can't charge it."

"You should have said, I would have loaned you mine."

"I kind of like the idea of telling her in person," I say, stepping out of my shoes.

My overnight bag has found its way in here. Another night, another room. Wonder if I'll ever get out of Noel Ridge.

"It'll be a really nice Christmas gift for her." Eve sits on the edge of the bed, wrapping her arms around herself. She fiddles with the bracelet on her wrist that her dad gave her.

"It's cold, Eve. You should get into bed."

She nods, then goes to use the bathroom. I grab my sweatpants and quickly change into them, tossing my shirt into the bag, but leaving the t-shirt on, I wait for her to finish. She comes out and looks at me in my makeshift pajamas.

"Do you want a hot drink before bed?"

"Uh, probably not coffee and that tea was..."

"We have hot chocolate," she laughs. "You didn't like the tea?"

"It was okay, just not my thing."

"Go get washed up and I'll make the drinks. Feel like a movie? I'm not tired yet."

"So long as it's not a Christmas movie."

"Are you a grinch, Dash?" she smirks.

"It's been said once or twice," I wink and go into the bathroom.

After using the toilet and washing my hands and face, with freezing cold water, I come out of the bathroom to find Eve propped up in the bed. Two steaming mugs sit on each bedside table. The TV is on too, casting more light into the room.

Ridgewood was right about keeping everyone warmer. The padded red quilt looks like an air mattress, it's so thick.

I'm not gonna complain. It's damn cold in here now. Eve pulls back the covers for me and I hurry over and get in. The sheets are cold, and I hiss. Eve laughs.

"It warms up quick."

There is something wildly domestic about this bedtime routine we're enacting. I've lived with a woman before. For three years. I'm no stranger to having a woman around. This is different. I pick up the hot chocolate and take a drink. It's the same mix from downstairs and is delicious.

Eve has chosen an action-adventure movie over a Christmas one, or a rom-com. Guess she figured I wouldn't like one of those either. We sit propped up on our own sides of the bed, the covers pulled up to our chests.

The silence lengthens. This isn't us. We've usually always got something to talk about. Maybe she's still upset after the call with her dad.

"How did your Christmas Eve, eve tradition start?" I ask, setting my mug down and pulling my arm back under the covers. My shoulder feels like it's frozen from being out in the cold air.

Eve sets her drink down and ducks under the covers too, pulling them up to her chin. She rotates slightly so she is on her side facing me.

"It started in dad's family because his dad often worked away on the holidays. He got paid more. Dad has five brothers and two sisters so they needed the money. When I was a kid, I thought it was all about me," she smiles. "Holly never let me get away with that," she adds. "Dad probably shouldn't have done it, but he always winked at me after Holly complained. Then he'd chase us around and hug us both to let Holly know it was just as much hers as mine. That wink though, I always knew it really was a secret just for me and dad.

"Then I got older and realized it really was just a coincidence that my name matched up with the tradition," her smile falls a little.

"I always go to Daria's on Christmas Eve. Dad too. She has two kids."

"You're going to get home in time for that," she assures me.

"I don't know, I've been invited to the wedding now."

Eve laughs. "They don't expect you to stay, Dash. You have a family to get home to."

She shivers again and then yawns so big her jaw cracks. It's been a long day, for both of us. And she's not had the best of times with finding out about her parents.

"It was great news about Henrickson, Dash. You should be proud of yourself. Not only did you impress him, you got him to offer to take you on for all of his future work."

"It hasn't sunk in. And I don't think I'll fully believe it till his office gets in touch."

"I've already said this. He wouldn't have driven out of his way, in this awful weather, if he didn't mean it." She touches my arm.

Her hand is freezing. I reach out and take it between mine, rubbing it to get it warm. She goes quiet and watches me.

"It's cold." I expect one of her sarcastic retorts but instead she shuffles a little closer.

"You know what they say about body heat."

"Shared body heat?" I ask.

Her head bobs. I let go of her hand and lift my arm so she can scoot underneath it. Eve rests her head against my shoulder, and I pull her against me. We lay like that for a while, watching a movie I have no fucking interest in. All of my attention is on the body pressed into mine.

She moves her leg so it's resting over my thighs. We still haven't talked about yesterday. I felt like a coward leaving without talking to her. It seemed like the right thing to do at the time.

Eve hasn't argued with me once, or even brought it up.

Yet here we are, in a bed together, her tits are pressed against my side, the warmth of her thigh pressing into mine.

"You know that whole body heat thing," I murmur.

Her hand slips under my t-shirt. "Skin to skin works best?"

My cock lengthens. It's taking all my self-control not to roll her over and slam inside of her. "Yeah."

"You're right."

Eve pushes my t-shirt up, exposing my abs and chest. When she ducks under the covers and lifts it higher, my pulse spikes. Then her lips touch my body and I can't fucking stand not touching her any longer.

I help with my t-shirt, pulling it over my head. Eve crawls over me and I spread my legs so she can fit between them. My head is still outside, but I lay back and enjoy the feel of her hands roaming over my skin. Hot wet kisses follow in their wake, and I groan as her hand pushes inside my sweatpants.

The lump under the covers almost makes me laugh, it's like we're teenagers hiding what we're doing in case we get caught. My pants move and I shift a little to help her get them down over my thighs. I should get under the covers too. Not being able to see her is exciting me even more.

My cock is throbbing painfully, desperate for her touch but she's gone still. I'm about to ask what is wrong when her tongue moves up the length of me. My head tips back on the pillow and I groan. She licks me again, circling around the head and then moving back down the underside of my cock.

"Fuck," I growl out, wanting more.

Eve doesn't disappoint. Her mouth closes over my tip and her tongue swirls around the opening, tasting my pre-cum. My hips jerk, making my cock disappear further into her mouth.

"Sorry," I force out.

She responds by sucking more of me in, swallowing me as far as she can go. Damn I want to see her. I lift the covers, the cold air makes me shudder. The little light from the candle is enough for me to see her blonde hair. It's covering her face as she bobs up and down on me.

"Jesus your good at that," I moan.

She can't answer with a mouth full of cock, so she licks me again as she moves up and lets out a moan. That sound has me on the verge of losing my load. When her hand closes around my balls I nearly do, thrusting up, unable to stop myself.

"Eve, I'm gonna come," I warn her.

She doubles down, gripping the base of my cock and working the length faster. The mixture of her hot mouth, her tongue and her hand movements push me over the edge. I growl and curse as I come down her throat. My body flops back onto the bed, my chest heaving and heart hammering.

I don't usually finish in someone's mouth, always pulling out, or stopping before I get to that point so I can put my cock inside.

She's still gently licking me, swirling her tongue around my head. This time I push the covers back so I can see her as she licks away the last of the cum. It's the hottest fucking thing I've ever seen in my life.

How I'm not going to be able to see this woman again almost takes me out of the moment. Then she sits up on her knees and pulls her top off. All those worries disappear.

Her nipples peak immediately from the cold. I sit up and cup her breasts, pushing them together and dipping my head to have a taste. Eve clutches the back of my head as I give her tits the same treatment she gave my cock. She must like it because she is moaning, panting, and writhing her pussy over my cock.

Access is easy because she is wearing loose shorts. I move my hand inside the waistband, underneath her panties and find her wet, almost dripping.

"Need you on my cock," I say against her ear, biting on the lobe.

"Yes," she puts her hand between us and starts working it.

It's not getting as hard as before because I just came but she doesn't give up, still thrusting against me as she works. Riding my hand, she takes her own pleasure.

Her head drops back, and her eyes squeeze shut. Goosebumps are springing up all over her and the draft on my back is cold as hell. I don't stop, stroking her clit hard as I push a third finger into her.

"Oh God," she cries out and then moans as my fingers are squeezed tightly together. "Dash," her breathy voice has my cock finding its second wind.

I sit up higher, pulling my hand out and push her off me. Her pants are gone in seconds and I duck down licking away her release. I've never wanted a woman so bad in all my life. But I don't have any condoms.

"I do, they're in the drawer."

Fuck, I said that out loud. Doesn't matter, she's solved the problem. I crawl up her and open the drawer, there are three condoms inside. I raise a brow at her and she shrugs. I would have been gone though so...

"Dash, it's cold."

"Sorry."

I forget about why she got them and pull the covers completely over us, so we're plunged into the dark and warmth. Her hands are everywhere, running over my shoulders, my chest, down around my waist and hips. I lift up and rip open the condom. Eve helpfully holds my cock for me as I slip it on.

Then I'm pushing inside. Not being able to see her irritates me but there is something more exciting about it too.

The urge to move isn't as strong as earlier, so I thrust slowly. Finding her mouth, I kiss her, matching the tempo of my tongue with the thrusts. We kiss the whole time, connected in every possible way. I'm starting to sweat as the heat beneath the double layer of blankets builds up, but we stay like that.

We fuck slow, our kisses turning from frantic to more of an exploration. This is even better than the first time. Her legs wrap around me, and a slight breeze comes in where the covers have lifted.

It's a welcome reprieve but still I keep us covered. Not being able to see has heightened all my other senses, touching her, tasting her, smelling the scent of sex, it's driving me wild.

My thrusts get harder, but still slow. Eve clutches my shoulders and bites my earlobe.

"Fuck," I groan.

"Keep doing that," she whispers, and I thrust even harder, pushing so far inside her it feels like I'll never come back out. "Yes. Oh God. I'm gonna come, Dash. Harder. Fuck me harder."

Hearing her say my name drives me wild and I move faster. I take both of her hands and push them up above her head, outside of the covers, trapping them so she can't move. I pound harder, pressing up slightly to get more leverage with my knees in the mattress.

She moans and cries and thrashes, her hands trying to break free. But she's pinned down. Faintly I can hear the bang of the headboard against the wall, and it spurs me on. I find her mouth as my body starts to let go, swallowing her final moans as she reaches her climax.

I follow quickly after, my head blacking out for a moment as the orgasm goes on and on. We lay still, coming down from the high.

"Can you get the covers, I can't breathe."

I laugh and kiss her then peel the covers off our head, releasing her hands. Her face is all red and sweaty, her hair is a wild mess, but nothing could be sexier to me. Knowing I did that to her.

"That was," she breathes out heavily.

"Yeah," I kiss her cheek then pull back, stroking more hair from her face and neck. "You're beautiful," I say before she can make a comment about how she must look.

Eve swallows her words and smiles softly at me. The moment stretches as I stare into her blue eyes, feeling things that I can't decide if I want to run from, or hold on to and never let go.

The condom makes the decision for me, it's so fucking full. Making quick work of it, I run to the bathroom. Once it's tied off and in the trash, I run back. My cock and balls have shriveled just from that quick dash to and from the bed.

Eve laughs as I get back into bed, then squeals when I put my cold body against hers. "Oh my God how did you get so cold so quickly?"

"Because it's colder than a snowman's ass crack out there," I grin. "Warm me back up," I grab her and roll onto my back, pulling her over me as she laughs at my comment.

She lays her head against my chest, her hair tickling my jaw. I brush it aside then rest one hand on her head, the other on her lower back, as though I'm stopping her from ever getting off me.

"We were supposed to build snowmen today," she says, her lips moving against my chest.

"Why didn't you?"

"Holly."

My fingers make slow circles on her lower back and she sighs, comforted by the movement.

"I've never made a snowman before."

"Then you should make one tomorrow."

"I take it you're an expert."

"Well, you know."

"Of course," she laughs again.

We lay there quietly. The TV is still playing and is the only sound in the room. A God damn Christmas movie is playing.

"Dash?"

"Yeah?" I say it as quietly as she said my name.

"I'm glad I met you."

It's not exactly what I thought she was going to say, and I let out a sigh that is part relief and part disappointment. "Me too," I kiss the top of her head.

"And..."

"What?" I hold my breath.

"You need to blow out the candle in the lantern."

"Fuck," I grunt. "I think you should do it. I already had to get out once."

"Rock, paper, scissors?"

"No. Move your ass woman," I slap her ass, and she yelps out a laugh.

Sitting up, I watch as she scurries out of bed and opens the small glass door in the lamp. Her body is fucking beautiful. I've been with all kinds of women in my life and never had any complaints about any of them, no matter their size.

Eve's skin is smooth as silk, her ass is round and full, tapering to her narrow waist and flat stomach. She has the best tits I've been lucky enough to get my hands on. She glances at me as I stare. Without turning her gaze from me, she blows out the candle.

The smaller one by me isn't casting much light now that it's burned down so much. As Eve climbs back under the covers, I turn off the TV and blow it out so we're plunged into the dark.

This time, I move into her, pushing my front to her back and tuck the covers in around us. I kiss where her shoulder meets her neck and she sighs.

Funny, this feels a whole lot more intimate than us fucking. In my head, I know it wasn't just fucking.

It was so much more.

Chapter 15

Dash is sleeping soundly beside me when I wake. For some reason, I'd been expecting him to have left and a thrill races through me that he is still here. It's too cold to prop myself up and watch him, not to mention weird. My eyes can't help but take in the beauty of his face.

His facial hair has been growing in over the last few days. Guess he didn't think to bring a shaving kit, given he was only supposed to be in the area overnight, not all this time.

My heart twists remembering what I said to him. That I was glad we met. Thank God he said it back. That could have been weird. I'm glad I told him. The disappointment I felt yesterday at us not saying a proper goodbye stung.

If the blackout hadn't happened, he would have been gone and that stirs unease in me.

What are we doing? I'm catching feelings for this man, I know I am, even if I can't admit it.

It's going to be hard to say goodbye, especially after last night. He might have worked me over hard but something else happened. I imagined what it would be like if this continued.

That will never happen. We live so far away from each other. This has been a moment in time. An amazing one. I lay back and close my eyes. Why couldn't Ashlynn have just got married back home.

The thought doesn't sit right. As hard as it's going to be to say goodbye to Dash, meeting him and being with him is a memory I'm going to hold in my heart.

Jesus, what am I thinking?

He grunts and rolls over slightly, his head turning my way. I pause, holding my breath but he doesn't wake. Thankfully, I get to stare at him a little longer. I doubt he feels the same. It hurts my heart to think he might only see this as a crazy few days where everything went wrong, but he got to have some good sex, with a stranger he'll never see again.

Are we strangers though? I flop back on the bed, trying to silence these stupid thoughts.

Ashlynn is getting married today. As her maid of honor, she needs me. I won't have time to spend with Dash. When we leave this room today, it really will be over.

Tears sting my eyes. I quickly blink them away, feeling like an idiot.

I need to remove myself from this situation. Pushing off the covers I start to sit up but Dash grabs my arm and pulls me back.

"Hey," I protest.

"Too cold, stay in bed."

God how I wish I could. He opens his eyes and sleepily rubs them then pushes a hand through his hair.

"Ashlynn needs me in her room. We have to start getting ready."

"This early?"

"Yeah, it's what brides do, it's a whole thing."

He nods but pulls me against him, anyway. Relishing it, just for a few moments longer I push my face into his neck. He cups the back of my head and I can't help but wonder what is going through *his* head right now.

Is he having the same internal struggle? Probably not, men are built different to women. I want to ask him when he's leaving but I bite my tongue. Dash leans back slightly and looks down at me. He trails his fingers across my cheekbone, along my jaw and his thumb gently strokes over my lower lip.

So, this is what heartache actually feels like.

He kisses me. I let him, reciprocating even though it makes me feel worse. My eyes squeeze tighter as we deepen the kiss. I feel how hard his cock is between us, but figure that is just a biological thing, nothing to do with being pressed up against me.

I'm growing wetter though the more he kisses me and the urge to mount him is so strong. Dash has no such hesitation. He rolls me onto my back and slides his hand between my legs. I spread them without thought and before my brain can catch up with my body, he's sheathed himself in a condom and is sliding inside me.

We hold each other tight, and he kisses me a few times before burying his face in my neck. It feels bittersweet but I let my body succumb to the pleasure and cry out, for what I know, is one last time.

When he goes to clean up, pulling on his sweatpants and t-shirt I stare at the ceiling.

I only notice Dash standing in the doorway to the bathroom when he clears his throat.

"The hot water is back on."

"Great," I smile. "That must mean the power is back." I sit up and flip the switch on the lamp and it turns on. "Ashlynn will be disappointed she can't have a candlelit wedding."

"But she'll be able to shower," he wiggles his brows. "Which er, I probably should."

"Okay, you go first."

"Thanks," he disappears into the bathroom and closes the door.

I roll over and bury my face in the pillows. I wait until the shower starts to actually scream into it. My phone pings while he is showering. It's a ridiculous amount of happy face, flower and bride emojis. From Ashlynn obviously. I send back a few hearts then sit up.

The room isn't as warm as it has been but it's not 'freeze your ass off cold' like last night. Pull yourself together, you have a job to do today.

Dash comes out of the bathroom dressed in his jeans and shirt, rubbing a towel over his wet hair. "All yours," he says. "It's amazing how easily you can forget what a hot shower feels like."

I smile and get up. His eyes run over me and I remember I'm naked. Holding my head up high I walk towards him. He sidesteps but as I'm about to pass, he catches my waist and leans in to kiss my temple.

That somehow makes me even sadder. I move past him into the steam-filled bathroom.

"Do you have time to grab breakfast?" he calls.

"Um, I'm not sure if Ashlynn has something planned."

"Oh, okay. Well, I'll be down there, if you can make it."

"Okay," I call back, a little too breezily.

"Eve," he appears in the doorway before I can close it.

I have a towel pressed to my front like some kind of pointless shield. This man has touched every part of me.

"Do you want me to leave?"

"That's up to you, I mean, you want to get home to your family. You have a lot of big news to tell them."

"That isn't what I asked."

His stare is so intense I feel my knees buckle.

Stay. Don't leave me. Ever.

"I'm gonna be caught up in the wedding stuff. It'd be sweet of you to stay for Ashlynn and Carter. They really like you."

What? I really like you. Dash stares at me a second then nods. Did he want me to ask him to stay? Lord, I don't know. He turns away and starts to pack his things.

I push the door shut and lean back against it, holding the towel pressed between my breasts. My heart is thumping so hard I'm pretty sure Dash can hear it. This reaction is crazy. Really. I can't have fallen for a guy in the space of five days. It's just the romance of it all, the wedding, the cozy inn.

God is my life turning into a romance story?

Ashlynn won't mind if I have breakfast with him. In fact I'm sure she'd push me to. I swipe a hand through my hair and look in the mirror. Jesus, what a mess.

That doesn't matter. What matters is letting him know that I wish he didn't have to go, but know he does. It's gotta be better than what just happened.

But when I pull back the door, the room is empty.

Ashlynn is like a whirling top, unable to sit still, checking in on everyone, running over everything again and again. All completely understandable. Despite it all, she is practically glowing.

Against all the odds, the wedding planner made it this morning and has, to the best of her ability, taken over.

Our breakfast was delivered to the room. As I nibble on some toast, I wonder if Dash is downstairs alone. Probably not, he fit right in with everyone here. He'll likely be surrounded by people.

That are not me.

I need to snap out of this. So, I smile and join in and finally remember the gift dad gave me to give to Ashlynn. I hurry back to the room to get it. As I'm leaving, mom is coming out of her room two doors away. She turns to see who it is and her face freezes.

It would be rude to just turn and walk away, even if that is what my whole body is telling me to do.

"Morning Eve," mom says a lot quieter than she normally speaks.

"Hey."

She glances at the gift in my hand, the curlers in my hair and my pj's which Ashlynn said we all had to be dressed in to get ready.

"How is Ashlynn this morning?"

"Nervous. Happy."

Mom nods and swallows hard. She goes to speak again but I hold up the gift.

"I've got to get back with this. Ashlynn and her planner need us all there."

"Oh, yes. Of course. Tell her I'm thinking of her and can't wait to see her."

It's on the tip of my tongue to say dad would have loved to see her too, but you ruined that. I bite it instead and just turn away. It pains me to turn my back on my mom, but she brought this on herself. How she thought this wouldn't affect Holly and me too, I don't know.

Back in Ashlynn's room, I hand over the gift. When she pulls it out, it is another bracelet the same as the ones we got, inscribed to her, love Uncle Jack. She puts it on immediately, not caring if anyone thinks it doesn't match. She holds up our arms and asks for someone to take a picture to send to him.

Then as the chaos continues, she presses her forehead to my temple.

"Are you okay?"

"I'm fine. Let's not worry about me, this is your big day."

"But I do worry. A lot has happened over the last few weeks. I know you miss your dad."

"He's here in spirit."

"Is there something else you're upset about?"

"I'm not upset. I'm overwhelmed, I don't know how you're coping with all this going on."

I indicate the hair and make-up people, the planner on her cell phone and Ashlynn's mom passing out food. She keeps saying she doesn't want any of us to feel sick off of an empty stomach.

"You know I thrive on chaos," she smiles. "Did things go okay with Dash last night?"

"Fine."

"One word."

"I could give you a full description if you'd like."

"Maybe later I'll hold you to that."

"Ashlynn, it's time for your hair."

"Just a sec," she says to the planner. "Eve, is he leaving today?"

"You know he is. He's got a family to get back to and amazing news to share with them. He probably can't wait to get out of here."

Ashlynn's lips pout out and she sighs. "Oh honey," she pushes some of the loose hair over my shoulder. "Maybe this was the wrong time and place, but it doesn't have to be the end."

"I appreciate the romanticism and your enthusiasm but please don't."

Whatever she sees in my face, it stops her from pressing the point. She paints on a smile and pulls me into a hug. "I'm here for you."

"I know. Now let's get you beautiful."

I shove her towards where a chair is set up in front of a large mirror. Of course they have the honeymoon suite which is double the size of everyone else's room. Music starts to play as everyone gets more excited. I perch on the edge of the bed and join in. But Dash is never far from my stupid head.

Ashlynn's dad popped in at one point and started to cry when he saw her in the dress. It set off a few of the others but Ashlynn just beamed at him. She's saving her tears for the ceremony I'm sure.

My dress has a small train but not as long as Ashlynn's. She wanted my dress to be slightly different to the others. I lost count of how many fittings we had. Mostly, because Ashlynn enjoyed being dressed up. Fortunately, I don't tend to have weight fluctuations, so my dress fits like a glove.

Just before I'm due to get into it, I tell Ashlynn I have something to do. She gives me a look, then blows me a kiss. In my room, I tug a hoody on over my pajamas and slip my feet into my boots. It's faster than getting changed. Luckily everyone here knows me.

Downstairs, I look around at the flurry of people moving in and out of the inn, mostly staff preparing the back patio for the ceremony. It's nice enough for us to hold it on the patio which makes me happy for Ashlynn.

In the bar and dining room I say hi to a few people and get stopped to ask how she is doing more than once.

I know who I'm looking for, but I can't admit it to myself. And I push away the disappointment of entering every room and not seeing him. He's probably long gone. I didn't exactly give him a reason to stick around.

When I step out onto the patio, I smile at the beauty of it. They've pulled glass shutters over the opening in the rails to close the space in and keep the cold out. You can still see out over the views though.

It's like a fairytale out here, with lights strung around the windows and Edison lamps hanging from the ceiling. The fire pit has been moved so that it isn't right in the center of the space.

The flowers are perfect, and there is a cream-colored carpet that has been laid out as an aisle. It smells like cinnamon apples and pinecones. The Christmas tree in the corner is professionally decorated, something no mere mortal would ever be able to achieve.

It doesn't look like the same space at all. She's going to be amazed and so happy when she sees all of this. I walk to the door that leads outside. It's freezing and I'm not exactly dressed for it, but I pull open the door and slip outside, huddling my arms around myself.

There are mushy footprints and inn workers are moving things around. They glance over at me, and one approaches to ask if there is any problem, but I say no, I'm just getting some air. He kindly offers me a coat, which I'm not too proud to accept.

One more night and then it's back to reality. I never dreamed I'd have as much fun up here as we did. Even with all the catastrophes. And even if they mostly happened to Dash and not the actual wedding plans.

I can't help but smile as I think about the snowball sled races. My mind goes to our kisses in the snow. God, I'm just torturing myself. I have to get back.

Turning around to trudge through the snow I stop short. He has his hands in the pockets of his thick jacket and is wearing his woolly black hat over his dark hair.

He stares at me in my weird outfit and frowns. He's probably going to tell me to get inside before I catch my death of cold, but that isn't what he says.

"Do you have time to build a snowman?"

Chapter 16

For a moment, she stares at me like I've gone mad, then she smiles and her whole face lights up. The tension in my stomach lifts at the sight of that smile. Her outfit isn't going to work though.

"Do you actually have time?"

"Yes," she says quickly.

"Like that?" I indicate her pajamas.

"Uh... Give me five?"

"I'll get started."

"Don't do too much," she hurries towards me.

"Okay."

As she disappears inside, I blow out a deep breath.

Earlier, the rental company sent me a text offering me two options, either an eleven AM or five PM drop off. The wise choice would have been the morning one. It's a long drive back to Cheyenne. Daria and Charlie are expecting me.

I was at the bar drinking a coffee and trying to force myself to select the eleven o'clock option, when Carter sat down next to me. From the way he looked at my phone I figure he saw the message. I set it down on the bar top. Carter called over for another coffee which the server gets to making.

"Nervous?" I ask him.

"Not nervous. It's more like anticipation of what's coming."

"Is that a good or a bad thing?"

"It's a fucking fantastic thing," he says. "Marrying Ashlynn is the best decision I've ever made."

That's quite the declaration. I've never had that kind of feeling before. The total surety of wanting one person beside me for the rest of my life. There has never been anyone that fit the space for me.

An image of Eve fills my head, but I push it away. My half assed attempt at getting her to open up and say something, backfired spectacularly.

I've never been the kind of guy to play games but with Eve, it's like my brain has gone to sleep. Why didn't I just tell her I wish I didn't have to go? That under different circumstances... Maybe.

She shot me down when I offered breakfast. That was understandable at least. She does have a lot to do today.

Then I outright asked if she wanted me to stay. Her answer to that said everything. I thought it best to just get out of there, so that is what I did. And then I got the message about the rental and ended up procrastinating without knowing why.

"It's not exactly how I envisioned my wedding to be," Carter says, sliding his coffee in front of him after the server has set it down. "I'd do anything for her."

I run a hand over my jaw and stare into my coffee.

"You know you really are welcome to stay for the wedding."

"Thanks, but I should go."

Carter turns on his stool and contemplates me.

"What?" I side eye him.

"I met Ashlynn at a medical conference in Fresno four years ago."

"Okay," I answer.

"I lived out in California when we met."

"I didn't know that."

"Yeah," he picks up his drink and watches people moving around behind us. "We spent the whole weekend together, had a lot of fun," he waggles his brows. "And then she went back to South Carolina. And I stayed in Cali."

"Really?"

"Yeah. We talked sometimes. Never said it was anything official, and I dated another girl for a while. But the whole time, I kept thinking about her."

Where is this going? He's trying to draw parallels between what happened with him and Ashlynn, with me and Eve?

"It was another year before I took a transfer. Figured why not. Only when I got there, she was dating this other guy."

"So how did this happen," I nod behind me to the patio where he is going to get married in a couple of hours' time.

"I didn't give up."

"Good for you."

"Of course, it helped that the boyfriend was an asshole. When they found out just how much of a bastard he was, her family and friends got her away from him. Eve even confronted the prick."

I stare at him for a moment. He doesn't have to say it for me to understand. The guy was violent. That makes me feel murderous. What the hell was Eve doing putting herself in that situation.

Carter gives me a knowing look.

"Anyway, I gave it a few months, she needed the space. I let her know I was there for her."

"She knew you were in town?"

"Oh, I made sure of it," he grins. "But I let things happen naturally. And they did," he holds out an arm indicating everything around us.

He's not exactly hiding where this is going. "I'm glad that happened for the two of you. It doesn't always work out for everyone."

"Depends on the connection."

He makes eye contact for longer than is comfortable, getting his point across without saying a word. We're guys after all. Talking about our feelings and offering advice isn't something we do.

"I gotta go. Need to look hot for the Mrs." He chuckles as he finishes his coffee. When he looks at my phone, he taps the bar top. "Go with the five pick up. You've done nothing but take risks since you got here, what's one more," he slaps my back and walks away.

We've not exactly hidden that we've been spending time together. Plenty of people knew I was in Eve's room last night. I'm also more certain than ever that Ashlynn has been in Carter's ear. It doesn't come across like he talked to me because of Ashlynn though.

That felt more like it came directly from *him*. He's close with Eve and I'm sure doesn't want to see her hurt. Am I hurting her? Is it really my fault, or is there anything I can do to change it?

The long distance and almost two years wait for Carter to get his girl isn't something I envision myself doing. I'm gonna be incredibly busy if Henrickson does come through. How am I supposed to find time for a long-distance relationship with all that going on?

I pick up the cell phone and stare at the text message some more. More and more people are showing up, so I get off the stool, thank the server for the coffee and head out to the lobby. My bag is by reception. I ask the lady if I can just grab my coat and hat and head outside to the front of the inn.

When I turned my truck into this driveway five days ago, I never expected to still be here.

To have met an amazing woman who hasn't been far from my mind every time I've left her.

The spot where my truck broke down is covered with as much snow as the rest of the driveway now, like it was never there. I haven't heard from the garage yet. I should probably call them, but I know in my heart I've lost that truck.

Shit. I stomp down the stairs, careful not to slip. I walk along the driveway, putting some distance between me and the inn. And I call my sister. We've never been the type to have deep and meaningful conversations about relationships, but she's the closest person to me who could maybe understand.

I need her to tell me what the hell to do because I have no fucking clue. We talked for nearly half an hour.

And now I'm rolling up snow, like a lunatic, to make the base for a snowman. Waiting for the gorgeous woman who has infiltrated my head and my heart.

I chose the five o'clock pick up.

I stand at the back of the patio area, next to the firepit. A smile twitches my lip at the memory of Eve burning my shoes and tie in there. Which reminds me, everything she told me about my meeting with Henrickson, was likely what brought him to the door of the Ridgewood Inn.

Not all of it, I'm not that awestruck. My hard work speaks for itself. Still, I can't help but wonder if I went in there and gave the original pitch, would he have come calling?

Music starts, jolting me out of my musings and I watch as Helene and Derek walk onto the patio. Her dress is a floor length dark green gown, and she has a gold fur lined shrug over her shoulders, it ties loosely around her collar bones with a ribbon.

The space is warmed by upright outdoor heaters rather than the firepit but there is still a chill in the air, everyone has a coat on. It's different, yet perfect for the person I've come to know Ashlynn is.

My eye roams to Carter, standing at the front of the room. His hands are crossed in front of his stomach as he watches his brother and sister walk up the aisle. His older brother is standing behind him, acting as best man. They've braved only wearing their wedding suits.

He isn't paying me any attention at all, but he did give me one of his patented slaps on the back when he saw me coming onto the patio. It's clear what he thought about me staying. And it has nothing to do with him or his bride.

Next comes another bridesmaid, Jessa and one of Ashlynn's brothers.

My gaze strays out of the window to the huge snowman and I stifle a laugh. Eve doesn't like to do things by halves. It is at least five foot tall, and has a carrot for a nose, rocks for eyes, buttons and a smile. It's wearing a bow tie, instead of a scarf, to match the men in the wedding party.

Some of the guests laughed at it when they filed in. It looks like he's watching from outside.

When I turn back to the room, Eve is standing in the doorway with the last of Carter's brothers, their arms linked.

She takes my damn breath away.

Her dress is different to the others, the same dark green, but it shimmers as she walks, and clings to her body all the way down to her ankles. She isn't wearing a shrug like the others, showing off the capped lace sleeves and low-cut bodice. It is elegantly straight across the tops of her breasts, not showing any cleavage, but it's molded to them perfectly.

My eyes skim her up and down and land on her face which looks even more perfect than normal. Her hair is half up and half down, blonde curls trailing down her back. And she's holding a huge bouquet of white and red roses.

My breath catches in my throat when our eyes meet. She knew I was staying, so it's no surprise but there is a touch of it in her eyes. Like maybe she didn't believe me when I said I wasn't leaving till after the ceremony.

Her soft smile is aimed at me, and me alone. Until she's drawn back into her duties and turns to walk down the aisle. I barely even notice when Ashlynn enters. Everyone else does, lots of oo-ing and aa-ing about how beautiful she looks. I've yet to take my eyes off Eve. Ashlynn could be wearing a Santa hat and doing the hula hoop, I wouldn't notice.

My attention is briefly snagged when they're saying their vows and I realize I missed something because everyone laughs, including Eve. The whole time my brain is running through scenarios where this could work. I just can't get it figured in my head.

Staying has only prolonged how hard it is going to be to leave. If I'd gone earlier, at least Eve would have been caught up in the wedding and not be thinking about me. We didn't discuss what was said, or not said, in the bedroom this morning but my staying has made a statement.

Daria only asked me one question after I told her everything. How I feel at the thought of not seeing her again. The answer was 'like shit'.

Feeling like shit is something we could both get over once the shine wore off.

My head is killing me, going round in never ending circles. By the time Carter and Ashlynn are kissing one another I've almost run out three times. The only conclusion I can come to now, is to keep hold of her number, and see how things go once we go back to our respective homes. Chances are, it will fizzle out.

If it doesn't...

"Would you like a glass of champagne sir, to toast the bride and groom."

"What, oh sure thanks," I tell the man in the tux. He's carrying a tray of champagne flutes. I take one and practically down it.

"You needed that, huh?"

Eve stands in front of me. She looks stunning, ethereal and a little cold. I take off my jacket and wrap it around her shoulders. She rolls her eyes at me but doesn't shrug it off.

"Yeah, just the one though."

"You didn't even wait for the toast," she laughs.

Eve doesn't miss my eyes moving to the clock on the wall. Less than an hour till my car gets here.

"So I've-"

"Do you want-"

We do that whole both talking at the same time thing again. I tell her to go first and this time she doesn't argue.

"I think, we both know that something happened here this week. And if you feel the same way I do," she looks into her champagne glass, a frown marring her brow. "I don't know what happens next."

"That is about as clear as mud," I joke. She shrugs one shoulder not laughing but not angry either. "I get it. I feel it too."

Whatever happens, I don't want to talk about it with everyone around.

I suggest we go somewhere private just for a quick minute. Eve agrees. Everyone is still busy congratulating the happy couple. The next part of the ceremony won't be happening just yet. We slip out of the patio and walk through the lobby. I glance down the hall to the event room and lift a brow.

She gives me a knowing smile and leads the way.

We stand opposite one another in the aisle. Eve takes off my coat and passes it back. I toss it on the nearest chair.

"It feels like we're walking away from something great, but I don't see any way around it other than long distance, and when does that ever work out?" she garbles out in one long breath.

"It worked for those two."

"Carter told you?"

"Yeah, he was the one that convinced me to stay. I reckon he's as hopelessly romantic as Ashlynn."

She laughs a little. "It might have started similarly but Carter moved. They didn't get together properly till then. I don't think you're gonna move to South Carolina, Dash. And…"

"You won't move to Wyoming," I finish for her.

Her head shakes slowly. Her breath hitches a little and I step forward and pull her into me.

"Maybe the magic was only ever at the Ridgewood Inn," I say softly into her hair.

She sniffles and I hate that she's crying. Fuck I wish I didn't have to do this. I wish things could be different.

I pull back and take her chin in the palm of my hand, tipping her head up so I can see her. Her gorgeous eyes are swimming with unshed tears. When one trickles over, I catch it with the pad of my thumb and brush it away.

"I won't forget this," she says. "Or you."

Maybe in time we both will but I don't want to say that. I don't even want to think it.

My own throat is growing thick. What the fuck is wrong with me? Love. The word ricochets around my head but I cast it aside. It can't possibly be that.

"You should get back to the party."

Eve nods and wipes her eye, in that way women do, when they don't want to smudge their make-up.

"Good luck with Henrickson," she says after a few seconds of pulling herself together. "It's going to be an amazing partnership."

"Thank you. And thanks for everything you did in helping me get that."

"I didn't do anything," she shakes her head.

"We both know you did."

"Maybe I'll take some credit." Her lips twist and she looks at her hands. "I better go."

"I won't come back in, can you let everyone know that I'm really grateful for what they did for me this week. I would have lost my mind if they hadn't all been so welcoming."

"I will."

"Take care, Eve."

"You too, Dash."

I take a step back, but I'm drawn to her. I can't help it, so move back in, taking her waist and bending to kiss her. Her arms wrap around my neck and for a few sweet, blissful moments, we kiss. Our last and final goodbye.

Eve leaves the room first. She doesn't look back.

I drop into the nearest chair and curse every fucking thing in existence, because I am never going to see her again.

Chapter 17

New Years Eve

"Earth to Eve."

A hand waves in front of my face. I swat it away and glare at my friend Jodi.

"Come on, there is only two minutes until the countdown. Why are you hiding in here?"

"I'm not hiding." I am. "I'll be there in a second, I just need the bathroom."

I don't, but I get up and head towards it. Leaving everyone to trail out onto the huge balcony for the imminent firework display. No expense has been spared tonight.

The bar we're at is hosting an exclusive party for one of the companies I do marketing for. I'm surrounded by glamorous people in expensive suits and dresses, drinking expensive cocktails. All getting ready for the beginning of a new year.

I've never felt more out of place.

In the bathroom, I stare at my reflection in the mirror over the sinks. I look like the rest of them. Hair and make-up on point, shimmery little black dress that skims my cleavage and lands mid-thigh.

The number of times I've thought about texting Dash is bordering on stalker level. I haven't because what would be the point of making this situation harder? He hasn't contacted me either.

Nothing more could have been said that last time we were together at the Inn.

It's irrational and stupid and maybe a little over the top, but I've cried more than once over him. Like maybe every other night. Ashlynn is away on her honeymoon, and I have no intention of talking about him to my friends here.

Holly helped a little, dispensing advice that wasn't the bitchy, jealous laden rant it could have been. Nope, this is locked away inside my heart and that is where it will stay.

I wonder what he is doing tonight. God damn my treacherous brain. Stop it!

People outside start counting down. I can't be hiding in the bathroom, no matter how swanky it is, as the new year comes in. Taking a few deep breaths, I hurry into the crowd of people.

I smile and laugh and even let one of the guys give me a new year kiss. Just a peck, and then I back away.

All I can think is, who is Dash kissing right now.

March

Ashlynn sets my coffee down in front of me and cocks her head to the side.

"What?"

"You still have that look in your eye."

"No I don't," I argue. I haven't cried in two weeks now. I don't say that aloud though.

"What did you think of that guy Carter set you up with?"

"Uh, yeah he was great." I avoid making eye contact because she can read me like a book.

"You didn't even go," she lightly slaps my hand where it rests on the table. "Don't think he didn't tell Carter you made up an excuse." She sighs heavily. "Eve, you and I both know I'm a sucker for a good romance plot, but you both agreed that it was not going to work out."

"It is over," I roll my eyes.

"Is it? Really?"

"Leave it, Ash."

She sips her green tea. That isn't her usual drink. Ashlynn is a coffee fiend. My eyes narrow on her. She looks guilty about something. We stare at each other and her eyes sparkle.

"You're not."

"I am," she smiles.

"Oh my God!"

I jump up and she does too, and I pull her into a hug. We're both laughing and crying and everyone is looking at us like we're lunatics.

"When did this happen?"

"Working backwards, you won't believe this," she laughs. "It was on Christmas Eve, eve."

"You're kidding," I laugh. "And what the hell where you doing making a baby with Carter on Christmas Eve, eve. That was the night before the wedding. You swore you weren't going to see him."

"Well, the blackout was scary."

"My ass," I give her arms another squeeze and we sit back down. "You're going to make the perfect family. How is Carter taking it?"

"He's ecstatic. Although he's fluctuating between wanting a girl and a boy. And when it's a girl, he gets all growly protective saying she'll never be allowed to date boys. And if it's a boy of course he's going to be a firefighter."

"Sounds perfect to me."

We finish our drinks and cake and then Ashlynn links my arm as we walk back to our cars. There is something else on her mind. She'll get to it in her own time. I've learned to let Ashlynn get things off her chest when she's ready.

"So... I saw something in the news yesterday."

"Okay," I pull off my denim jacket and open the back door of my car.

I leave the door open to let some air in, which seems moot given the air outside is warm too. We're having a more moderately warm start to the season than normal. Not a drop of snow in sight here.

"Remember that guy who came to the inn, the millionaire from the big company?"

"Lewis Henrickson?"

"Yeah him. He's hot by the way. I thought that when I saw him but for obvious reasons didn't bring it up. Anyway," she goes on. "He's announced that his subsidiary company, or something, are building some new sustainable homes. It's big news."

"Really, I hadn't noticed."

"You're a big fat liar."

Okay, so maybe I have been keeping an eye on Henrickson Inc's website. And occasionally checking in on Dash's. Only because I want to make sure Henrickson came through on his promise to hire Dash's company.

"Now you know that he is working with them, his company is safe, doing big business and..." she trails off.

"I'm happy for him."

"I knew it was important to you that he did get the contract."

"Yep."

"Are you okay?"

"I'm fine Ashlynn," I take her hands. "I promise. Now let's forget about the past and focus on the future. Given this little one was conceived on Christmas Eve, eve. I think that means if it's a girl, it's gotta be called Eve, right?"

"Logic says so," Ashlynn smiles at me, but she is still staring at me, trying to figure me out.

I have to get better at hiding how I feel. When I get home, I devour all the articles about the new housing project. Especially the ones with photographs of Dash, and his sister.

He looks happy. He looks good. I'm happy for him.

May

I'm up to my eyeballs in paperwork, or computer work. I don't have paper anymore. Doing my best for the environment after all. A brief flash of memory threatens to take over my brain. I push it away.

I've tried really hard over the last couple of months not to dwell in the past. It's worked, for the most part. I have a date tonight. One I promised Ashlynn I would actually show up for.

I feel ready. I've got no intention of standing this one up. I only did that once and felt like shit afterwards. Any other dates I canceled in advance. Like that makes it any better.

He's a good guy. Not someone Ashlynn and Carter have set me up with. He's a chef who recently moved here from the UK. His accent is sexy as hell. He's good looking, has a great job and the man can cook. I've eaten at the restaurant where he works a few times now.

My brain hurts from all the numbers. My accountant isn't allowed to go on vacation anymore. I close the laptop and head to the shower to get ready for the date.

Michael is charming. He tells me he's traveled the world and decided to settle in Carolina because he followed a woman here, he admits sheepishly. It didn't work out. But he liked it so much, he stayed, and he got the perfect job as head chef at one of the best restaurants.

There is a vague faraway look in his eye when he mentioned the woman. Red flag alert activated. He's hung up on someone else. He's only been here for five months. That tells me everything.

Still, I let him bring me back to my place, and he comes in for coffee. We kiss for a bit but neither of us is really into it. I'm sure he is, more than me, because he wants to get laid. I still have the same problem of needing a connection.

So he leaves, saying he'll call. He won't.

And another one bites the dust.

August

Ashlynn looks like she has a beach ball under her pretty yellow summer dress. I've already told her twice she's glowing, and she scowled at me, telling me this is not a glow, this is sweat. She is sweating and hot and so ready for that baby to get the hell out of her.

Even Carter was surprised by that last outburst. He knows when to steer clear and when to offer comfort. Right now is a steer clear alert. It's left to me to calm down my cousin. We're at a cookout they're hosting for Carter's birthday. The usual suspects are here, as in the whole fire house, some of our family. Even Holly is here.

She's mellowed a lot since the revelations in Wyoming. Things with mom remain strained. Holly has given her more grace than me.

I'm trying. I just can't forget what she did. In my mind, it is worse than just cheating. Telling your spouse you're about to cheat and they should let you do it, then move on after you got it out of your system. It's just plain awful and makes my skin crawl every time I think about it.

"How many more weeks is it?" I ask absently.

At the silence I lift my head. Carter glares at me from across the yard, like I've lost my mind. Suddenly everyone is watching. I widen my eyes. I was too busy checking my messages to read the situation properly. Ashlynn's bottom lip quivers. Carter tips his head back and makes a face at me.

"Three, but that doesn't mean anything because your due date can be two weeks later," she wails and bursts into tears. Carter curses and comes over.

"Nice move," he mouths at me.

"Sorry," I mouth back.

He gathers Ashlynn up and gives her a hug and a kiss, steering her inside. Everyone stares at me in disappointment. Chase comes over and drops into Ashlynn's seat.

"You're supposed to be the one who can read her best. What's got you so preoccupied against your best friend slash cousinly duties."

"Nothing."

"Is it a dude?"

"No."

I've struck up an odd kind of relationship with Chase. He's way too young for me but we get along really well. He's like the younger brother I never had.

"You're too hot to be celibate."

"Chase, what have I told you about personal boundaries?"

"That I cross them with ease and very little care."

That is true. "It's not a guy."

"Show me then."

"Nope."

He lets out a laugh that sounds far too evil for his angelic face. "It's Gabe isn't it?"

"Do you ever give up?"

"Nah, you know I just want to see you happy."

I am happy. I am. Gabe is a really nice guy. We're getting along great and although I am indeed still celibate, not a hundred percent so. As in we've fooled around but not had full-blown sex. Whenever it gets to it, I always back off. I know it's frustrating him but he's being patient.

I'm frustrated with myself. I haven't thought about *him* in months. Okay, weeks. He just won't get out of my heart, no matter how much my head tries to shake him. I've stopped looking him up. His business was booming, the last time I did check. Henrickson has been the making of him.

He's even been in some environmental publications for the work he is doing. I'm so proud of him.

"I have to go," I say when I read the next text off Gabe.

"Go get it girl," Chase winks.

I don't dignify that with a response. But do yell bye to everyone in the yard and a chorus of byes and cheers come back at me.

Gabe picks me up at seven on the dot and we head to the restaurant.

While we eat, I stare at him as he talks, probably looking like I'm paying attention. What I'm actually doing, is counting up his attributes. He's smart, funny, good looking, fairly well off. He lives in my state, even my neighborhood.

How does that one always creep in?

Why won't I just let go and sleep with him? If I want this relationship to last it needs to go to the next level.

Men aren't the *be all and end all of human existence*, my conscience whispers.

I'm having a good time with Gabe. He makes me laugh, which is really important to me. Now, I guess we need to see if we're compatible in other ways. Enough for me to actually start thinking of him as my boyfriend.

The meal is lovely and I have a few glasses of wine, in the hopes of loosening up.

Namely my legs.

"Are you ready for the interview tomorrow?" Gabe asks as he drives us back to my place.

"I'm not worried. It's not like I need the business. I am kind of amused they want to interview me. It's usually the other way around."

"But it's a big deal. They have over a million followers on Instagram."

I shrug. I'm not all that bothered about big name clients or social media number count. I have enough to keep me busy. I only agreed to the interview because it intrigued me. My portfolio is enough to speak for itself, so I've not really put any preparation into it.

"You're gonna be great, they'll love you."

"Thanks," I smile over at him as he pulls up outside my house. My head is reeling with excuses for not inviting him in. So much for taking the next step. My thighs are gripping one another for dear life.

"You know what, maybe I do need to do some prep tonight. Do you mind if we end the night now? I promise I'll make it up to you."

He struggles to keep his face straight and I can see I'm losing him. Yet, I don't say or do anything to reassure him. What kind of asshole does that make me?

He kisses me on the cheek, and I get out of the car. He pulls away without making sure I make it into the house safely. What an ass. But I guess I brought it on myself. I can't blame him for driving out of here like he never wants to bother seeing me again.

"Eve, you are a mess," I say out loud. Closing my eyes as I wonder what is wrong with me.

"A mess?"

"Holy shit," I screech, grabbing my chest and turning around. I know that voice.

"I don't know Eve. You look pretty good to me. And that guy is an idiot."

My heart begins thrashing for other reasons. I blink a few times trying to make sense of what I'm seeing. On my front yard.

He's here.

Chapter 18

The last eight months of my life have been incredible. We've gone from a small family run business to a huge company employing over three hundred people.

Lewis made good on his promise and his assistant, Raine called me three days into the new year. Until it happened, I hadn't believed it was going to come off. What had been a miserable fucking new year turned into one of the most amazing phone calls I've ever got.

It's been a whirlwind since then. I went to so many meetings, met so many people, at first my head was spinning. Lewis has invested in the company rather than taking me on as an employee. He wants me to keep my autonomy, but he's giving me enough to conquer the world.

I was so busy I didn't have time to think about anything else.

Lewis is actually a genuinely nice guy, for a millionaire. He's as passionate as I am about the work we're doing. He wanted to grow the business as fast as possible. I managed to slow him down, to a degree. The biggest factor being I didn't have the workers he needed for so many projects. His response, just hire everyone I need and give him a figure. He said all the work I do for him will pay him back tenfold.

It was like all my Christmases came at once. And once we started working on the first project, I knew this is what I was born to do.

The only thing that could have made it better, was being able to share it with the woman I still feel was responsible for everything.

The number of times I almost called her bordered on insanity. The time I spent thinking about her nearly drove me mad. And the times I beat off in the shower. Well, let's just say my hand has got more action than I intended.

The only saving grace, I'm too busy for anything other than work. I don't have time for other women, and I was good with that.

And then Lewis suggested branching out of state. In fact, he wants to go global, but I reigned him in. Or at least told him that he would need another company under his umbrella to work on that. But the whole out-of-state thing intrigued me.

When we met to talk about it, I asked him how far out of our state he wanted to go. Given his desire for global domination, he said anywhere. He didn't care so long as he could help build the homes and buildings the planet deserved.

I kept my thoughts to myself for a while. It's been a long time since the Ridgewood Inn. I was sure she'd moved on. She's gorgeous, fun to be around, smart and... Perfect. Why wouldn't someone else have snapped her up.

So I let it go and we branched out into neighboring states, rather than going further afield.

Lewis invited me and Daria to all of his parties, where there were plenty of women who were more than willing to break my dry streak. I just wasn't interested.

It's my birthday today and Daria has thrown me a huge party. It's been going good, everyone is having fun. I got through the god-awful experience of having happy birthday sung to me.

Daria pulls me aside and asks what is going on with me. I have no idea what she's talking about.

"You haven't been the same since you went up to Noel Ridge."

"Don't be ridiculous," I tell her, drinking from my beer bottle.

The party is being held in my favorite bar. All my friends and family are here. And a lot of guys from the construction company. They spend a lot of time pranking each other and daring each other to do crazy shit that has my sister almost crossing herself.

They remind me of the firefighters.

Just another thing that keeps bringing my mind back to her.

"I'm not joking, Dash. You've thrown yourself into work since you got back."

"In case you haven't noticed, that is because it's a lot of work. I don't have time to slack off."

"You have people under you who can take on a lot of the responsibility. I know you're a control freak bro, but not as much as you have been these last few months."

"Doing this work means a lot to me. I want to be the best we can, and not disappoint anyone."

"Who exactly are you going to disappoint," she leans back in her chair and crosses her legs.

Sometimes I really wish I hadn't asked her for advice about Eve all those months ago.

"People," I mutter.

"I'm here to let you know that it's time to do something about it. Either move on, or go after her."

"Go after her? What are you talking about? I'm not having this conversation with you."

I get up and walk to the bar to refresh my beer. A prod to the shoulder tells me Daria has followed me. I roll my eyes and look back at her. Her arms are folded, and she's looking at me the way mom used to, when I'd done something that warranted a grounding.

"It's clear to me and even Charlie who never notices a damn thing. You're still hung up on her."

"Am not."

She rolls her eyes. "Are we really going to descend into talking like toddlers?"

"I'm not. You are."

"Don't be a dick."

"That's tremendously un-toddler like sis. Besides, she's probably with someone else by now. Won't even remember me."

"You'll never know, if you don't go and find out. You could ask Carter."

"I haven't talked to Carter in months."

We kept in touch, for a little while. Nothing heavy, it's not like we're friends but he let me know Ashlynn is expecting, and for a couple of months that Eve is still single. He stopped talking about Eve a while ago, which led me to believe she's dating someone else.

That pierced the wall around my stupid heart, but I brushed it off. We made our choice. What we had, stayed at the inn. Where it belongs.

"I had a chat with Lewis last week."

"About what?"

Thank God she is changing the subject before I have to take off my sock and stuff it in her mouth. I've done that before. It got her off my back for nearly a month, because she refused to speak to me.

Until now, she hasn't been pushy about the Eve thing.

The Eve thing. Jesus.

"Sites for a hotel."

"A hotel? He hasn't mentioned a hotel."

"He asked me to start designing something last week. He wants to start a chain. You know what he's like about expanding around the country."

Pinching the bridge of my nose, I let out a heavy breath. Talk about running before you can walk. Any little issue that arises, Lewis throws money at it. I guess I should be happy about that.

A couple of months into working with him I managed to buy myself a brand new, top of the line fully electric truck. It beat the hell out of the one I had before. I gave the go ahead to crush it when the mechanic in Noel Ridge finally got back to me.

"He will want you to oversee it."

"I'm working on the shopping center in Idaho right now. In fact, I'm going out there early next week for a while."

"Not anymore."

"What does that mean?" Now my arms are folded. We're like mirror images of each other, all riled up and not going to be the first to back down.

"It means, big brother, that I'm taking matters into my own hands. I've found an amazing piece of land just right for the flagship hotel."

My brow lifts. I refuse to ask any questions. Because I've reverted to middle school age tactics.

"It's in South Carolina."

"Excuse me."

"You heard me," she leans back against the bar and smirks. "And Lewis thinks it's a great idea. He has a condo in Charlotte. He loves the area. Said it's the perfect place for the first ever Henrickson fully eco-hotel."

"Even I know Charlotte is in *North* Carolina."

"Right next door."

My eye roll is epic. I must look like my thirteen-year-old niece. "I'll talk to him, there are other places we can start."

"Won't happen," she smirks even broader. "I told him you'd try to get out of it, and he couldn't let you."

"Tell me you didn't say it was about Eve."

"I might have."

"Fuck, Daria, this is our business partner, not some guy we've known for years who you can dump this crap on."

"He remembered her."

What? Oh, yeah, they met outside the inn. He gave her the once over. I'm sure he would have given her his number if I hadn't glared at him.

"I'm not doing this, Daria. Don't push it."

"You are doing it, even if you don't get your ass into gear and go see her. The hotel is going to be built in Columbia, South Carolina. End of discussion. Happy birthday." She leans in and kisses my cheek too fast for me to avoid.

I slam my bottle down on the bar as she walks away, laughing.

"Another?" the bar tender asks.

"Yeah, why the fuck not. Actually, make it a double shot of whiskey."

"You got it."

Carter meets me at a bar near the fire house. He's still got his work t-shirt on with the fire house logo but he's changed into jeans. He's on his break and can't drink alcohol but that is fine. I'll drink it for him.

"How many times have you been here now?" he asks with a grin.

After a begrudgingly long pause, I stare into my pint and mutter. "Five."

He laughs. "Man, this is bringing back memories."

"This isn't the same thing."

"How so?"

"I haven't spoken to her since Christmas Eve. You and Ashlynn kept in touch."

He scrubs his jaw, one elbow resting on the bar. We're in a quiet corner at least.

This *is* the fifth time I've been in Columbia. There really was no talking Lewis out of this location. And to be fair to him and Daria, the plot they found is perfect. The ball is well and truly rolling. We're about to start laying down foundations in the next couple of weeks.

And as lead engineer and construction site manager, Lewis wants me here to oversee everything. I can't even talk my way out of it because all the properties I've led on, I've been there to oversee.

It was on the third trip that I got in touch with Carter. He was shocked to see me, but happy. I made him swear on his unborn child's life he wouldn't tell Ashlynn. It was a dick move but Carter agreed, saying it was for a good cause.

"Man, all I'm gonna say is, if you want to make a move, you gotta do it this time."

"Why?" I ask, turning my head sharply to face him.

He gives me another one of those grins. "Because this recent guy, he's been around a few times."

Jealousy threatens to buckle me, or the glass in my fist.

"Don't worry, she tells Ashlynn everything, and she tells me. And you've got no competition. She's still hung up on you."

Seriously? I work hard to keep that question off my face. "That's ridiculous."

"Look. The way I see it, you're gonna be around for what, about six months while you get this hotel thing done. Can you really be in the same city as her for six months and not go see her? That's the first step."

I've purposely rented a place in Elgin, about thirty minutes outside of Columbia.

"Take it from someone who met and married the reason my heart keeps beating," Carter says, with a genuinely serious look on his face.

Damn, he's as bad as Ashlynn.

"I witnessed you guys together firsthand. You want to spend the rest of your life regretting this?"

"What if it doesn't work out?" I voice my fears.

"Then you go back to Wyoming, and we visit at Christmas when we head back up to Noel Ridge."

"You're planning to do that?"

"Yeah. Ashlynn thinks that every couple of years we'll make another baby on Christmas Eve, eve."

"There is seriously something wrong with you two."

He doesn't look in the least bit offended. "Whatever you decide, I'm here for you. Ashlynn will take care of Eve and if you decide not to contact her, they'll never know you were here."

Only if she doesn't follow what work I'm doing. That's a pretty big-headed statement to make.

Who's to say she ever thinks about me anymore.

"Chase has been keeping an eye on her. She's got a date tomorrow so you might wanna get in there before he does. Actually, we're having a cookout at my place, you should come."

"And spring it on her in front of everyone. No thanks."

"Moral support, back up, you know the guys at the fire house are rooting for you."

Yeah, he told them all I'm in town. All of them are sworn to secrecy. At this point, it's a miracle Eve doesn't know I've been coming to her home city for the last month.

"You're giving me a headache."

"You know what fixes a headache right up," he gives a filthy laugh and slaps my back. "Lots and lots of hot sex."

"Get the fuck back on shift," I push him off the stool.

"Keep me posted," he calls as he walks through the bar. People greet him as he passes, he has a wave and a smile for all of them.

The cookout was definitely out of the question. I wasn't even going to go try and catch up with her afterwards because she'd be on her date, but I found myself sitting opposite her house, in the dark, waiting for her to come home. I left the truck and went for a quick walk and a pep talk.

If she goes inside with the guy, then I'll back off. I'm not going to mess up her life if she's found happiness.

Why the fuck am I doing this to myself?

Just as I'm about to head back to my truck, a car pulls up in front of her house.

I duck behind a bush. I'm a fucking creeper, watching them as they talk. If there is a Home Owners Association or neighborhood watch here, I'm probably about to have the cops called on me.

Is he gonna get out and go with her? The longer they talk, the more it seems like he's not. The door opens and Eve gets out.

My breath catches at the sight of her. Her hair is longer, trailing down her back. She's wearing a dark-colored dress and heels, her arms and legs are bare. The only time I ever saw so much skin, was when we were naked together. As hot as she looks, I can't help but think about her all wrapped up in her puffy jacket and woolly hat.

The guy leaves. He doesn't even wait to see if she got into her house. He just drives away.

Fucking asshole.

Eve watches him go. Is she sad? Glad? Shit, what do I do?

"Eve, you are a mess."

That makes my blood boil. What the hell did he say to her? It also makes me show my hand. Because I don't want her to think that about herself. No matter what happens, she needs to know that she's fucking perfect.

"A mess?"

She almost jumps out of her high heels as she shrieks and spins around. "Holy shit!"

Eve is staring at me, her eyes blinking rapidly as she tries to compute what she is seeing. I take a couple of steps closer, my eyes roaming her body, then her face. Our eyes lock and I take another step.

"I don't know Eve. You look pretty good to me. And that guy is an idiot."

"What... how?"

"Did you just dump him?"

"Er... no. I mean, we're not really dating. Just," she rubs her forehead, completely flummoxed. "Dash, what are you doing here?"

Well, she said the magic words. That idiot doesn't know what he's losing out on.

Carter is right. Daria is right. I've missed her. She's the first thing I think of in the morning and the last thing at night. I beat myself raw fantasizing about her all the time. That last one doesn't need to be said aloud.

We've never been the best at communicating our feelings. We can talk and talk about everything else. We can show each other how we feel physically. But saying what we really feel. Yeah, not the greatest.

It's time we changed that.

"I woke my ass up."

"What does that mean?" Her voice is hopeful, laced with a hint of trepidation.

I walk over to her. Her chest rises and falls as she breathes heavier. Her eyes never leave mine.

"I've been an idiot. I should have done this months ago."

"Done what?" she whispers.

"Come for you."

"But, what about... Wyoming."

"It's early enough that we could book a room at the Ridgewood Inn for Christmas."

Her lips twitch, but there is still a touch of doubt in her eyes. "That isn't what I mean."

"Don't worry, I've got that figured out."

"You really mean that?"

"With everything I am. We'll probably have to compete with Carter and Ashlynn for the best room at the Ridgewood Inn though."

Her eyes widen in surprise hearing that. "How do you know that?"

"Because even though I stayed away, I never stopped thinking about you. And maybe I kept in touch with Carter every now and then."

Her mouth drops open. I decide to keep going before she gets into that.

"We were always meant to cross paths, Eve. I know that now."

I take her mouth with mine, gently, testing the waters. A part of me is expecting her to push back, to ask what the hell I'm doing showing up, saying all of this, thinking I can just kiss her.

But that doesn't happen. Her arms go around my neck. Eve opens her lips for me, her tongue tangles with mine. Telling me everything I need to know.

I won't let this pass me by again. I pull her flush against me and kiss the shit out of her.

"You've definitely dumped him," I growl out against her mouth, then kiss her again before she has a chance to respond.

Sure, we've got a lot to talk about. Plenty to figure out. I will do everything I can to make her realize this is it for me. I've been miserable since Christmas Eve, without Eve.

I'm in love with this woman, and I don't ever want to be with anyone else.

Carter was right. I get it now.

Eve Dalton is the reason my heart is beating. And she always will be.

Epilogue

"Do you really want to see it?"

"Call it morbid curiosity."

"You could just look it up online."

"What would be the fun in that?" Dash grins.

I don't make the turn onto the road that leads to the Ridgewood Inn, instead carrying on the extra miles toward Evergreen Hollow.

Nostalgia hit me when we got off the plane and picked up our rental for the drive to Noel Ridge. Only this time Dash is with me, we flew in from South Carolina together. We'll be making the journey to Cheyenne to see Daria and the rest of his family for Christmas day.

It's my first time meeting them in person and I'm valiantly trying not to be nervous. I'll worry about it nearer the time. We've spoken on a few of Dash's many video calls with Daria and I met Charlie and the kids that way. Still, nothing is the same as meeting your boyfriend's family in person.

It's snowing, as expected. There is no snowstorm forecast this year. Knowing our luck, anything can happen. We have packed nothing but sensible shoes.

As we draw nearer to the site of the hotel which started all of this a year ago, Dash groans.

A huge concrete and steel skeleton sits on the side of the road on the way into Evergreen Hollow. Dash is quiet as I pull over on the opposite side of the road to the site. I already know what he's thinking.

There is no animosity, no told you so on his face. He's upset. Work has stopped on the building, possibly for the holidays but in my heart, I know that isn't true. The site looks like it's been abandoned for a while.

"Lewis didn't tell you?"

"When he split away from Henrickson Inc, he left it all behind."

There had been some drama between Lewis and his father and uncle. Dash speculated it was because Lewis's new side of the business is thriving. Right or wrong, Lewis kept his family out of it. They want the money and reputation he is amassing. It isn't about the money for Lewis. He wants to make the planet a better place for future generations.

"Is your curiosity satisfied?"

Dash stares at the building some more and shakes his head.

"Maybe I can convince him to buy them out. It's not like he doesn't have the money and we have a team that can fix this. I hate seeing it like this. Evergreen Hollow is a beautiful town, it doesn't deserve this eyesore marring people's opinion of it before they even get there."

I hide a smile. This is awful obviously but I'm so proud of him. He's never lost his passion for what he does. It stands to reason his first thought is how he can fix it for the town. It isn't the best way to start our Christmas trip, but it will have played on his mind if we didn't check it out.

"Let's go," he says, without getting out. "Sorry, we shouldn't have driven all this way."

Reaching over, I squeeze his thigh. He needed to come, and I will always do what Dash needs.

"When are the others getting here?" Dash asks as we make the drive back to Noel Ridge.

"Christmas Eve, eve," I smile. There is a touch of melancholy to it because the family is still split.

Dad and Susan, his girlfriend, and Holly, and her new boyfriend Rory, are joining us. We couldn't miss Christmas Eve, eve again this year. When Dash floated the idea of coming to the inn, and inviting them along, I think I fell in love with him a little more.

He didn't forget the tradition.

Dad loves Dash. From the moment I introduced them they got on. They go out to dad's local bar every couple of weeks to watch the hockey.

Mom won't be coming. Our relationship has got better over the last few months. It's never been the same. We still see her regularly but there is always an underlying tension that we've never got over.

Unfortunately for her, she tried to have a relationship with the co-worker she slept with. It didn't last. I guess the shine of something different wore off pretty quickly when she figured out he is actually an asshole. If ever the lesson the grass isn't always greener was learned.

The last four months have been an absolute whirlwind but amazing at the same time. When Dash showed up in Columbia, I had no idea he'd be working there. It took me a while to believe he was even standing on my front path.

Then Dash kissed me, and everything made sense. Those eight months without him, I was just existing. Going through the motions, doing what I thought people wanted of me. Finding someone else was never going to work. Dash Miller somehow worked his way inside my heart in those short five days at Noel Ridge. Nothing, or no one else can replace him.

He kept his rental in Elgin for about a month before moving in with me. Even if it is temporary.

That was a transition for both of us, but I went into it with an open mind. Now I don't want him to leave. He still has a lot of work to do on Lewis's hotel so it can be put out of my mind for now.

One thing I do know, whatever happens, or wherever we end up, it will be together.

Ashlynn and Carter had their baby boy a couple of months ago. She has been so busy with him we've not spent much time together. The baby is absolutely adorable, and I was over the moon when she asked me to be his Godmother.

When we do see them, she complains we care more about the baby than her. Carter is just pleased to get some adult time with another guy who is happy to drink beer with him while someone else watches the baby. Not that he doesn't adore the little bundle of joy.

Being so preoccupied most of the time didn't stop Ashlynn telling me she '*told me so*' when she found out Dash came to South Carolina for me. Not that I cared about her gloating. I'm glad her *feeling* wasn't broken.

Because of the baby, they're not coming up to Noel Ridge this year but have plans to return next year. Which means we get the best room in the inn.

It's odd not to see my family here. The few people milling around are nice enough but keep to themselves.

I wonder if we should get the people in the room next to us some earplugs…

I'm drawn out of my thoughts descending into getting my boyfriend naked, by a big cheery greeting.

It's Bernard, who remembers us by clicking his fingers and calling Dash 'ankle'. I burst out laughing but Dash isn't overly happy of the reminder.

"It brought us closer," I whisper in his ear, as Bernard grabs our key.

He gives Bernard a withering look, which I counteract with a grin and a wave. I grab Dash's arm and drag him away. We don't need directions.

"Reduced to body parts," Dash grumbles as we head to our room.

"And not even the best ones," I wink at him.

He gives me that look that makes my thighs clench. Yeah, before we do anything else I'll be getting him out of those clothes again.

Dash knows exactly what I'm thinking as he crowds me at the door. He pushes against my ass, nuzzling and kissing the small area of bare skin on my neck, between my coat and woolly pink hat.

He never fails to send shivers through my body. Be it with a look, a touch. Or getting home after a long day, picking me up wherever I am, no matter what I'm doing, to carry me to the bedroom.

We enter the room and stop dead, staring at the bed.

"Did you ask for this?" I glance at him.

"Me? No," he wrinkles his nose.

Dash is romantic in his own way. He takes care of me in all the ways that matter, more than making grand romantic gestures. This isn't something I see him doing. I *definitely* didn't arrange it.

"I can guess who did though," he laughs.

The bed is covered in rose petals. A bucket with champagne and two glasses is set up on one of the bedside tables. There is a note propped against the bucket. Dash sets down the bags as I read the note.

Dear Dash and Eve,

We hope you have as wonderful a time at the Ridgewood Inn as we did last year. And who knows, maybe you'll make a little friend for James. This place and this bed have very special powers. Enjoy!

Merry Christmas to our favorite people in the world.

All our love,
Ashlynn and Carter

My heart thumps and I turn to Dash.

He is unbuttoning his coat. "I'm starving, do you think they have those cinnamon pancakes? We can order up and I'll drizzle maple syrup all over your ti..." He lifts his head and looks over at me trailing off. "Why do you look like you've seen a ghost?"

I hold the card out to him, and he reads it quickly. His head comes up fast and we stare at each other. Dash shudders as he looks back at the bed.

And this is why I love him with all my heart.

Without a word, we grab our bags and head back downstairs.

Luckily, this time, there is a free room at the Ridgewood Inn.

Acknowledgements

When I started writing this book, I didn't think it would be released, especially not this fast. Dash and Eve just flowed right out of me. I've watched so many Christmas romance movies lately that I got inspired.

Christmas is one of my favorite times of year, being with family and friends. Falling in love! I wanted to write something uplifting and spicy so I really hope you enjoy it, lovely readers. It would make me so happy if you could take the time to leave a review, big or small, it all counts.

While I was writing this, I suffered some personal tragedies, losing both my cousin and my best friends' mum, very unexpectedly within a week of one another. This book is dedicated to my beautiful, selfless and open hearted cousin, Nancy. Mum of four, daughter, sister, aunty, cousin, niece. She was loved by everyone she met, a truly beautiful human. And so very talented. She wrote her own book and I was in the process of helping her navigate the self-publishing world. I'm going to miss her.

As always, a huge thank you to my Beta readers, Sandra and Karen. Especially given I've bombarded them with so many books this last few weeks. They do a sterling job and I'd be lost without them.

To my two best friends in the whole world, Gary and Graham, they've kept me laughing and loving life for nearly 25 years now and I hope it continues for many more.

Thank you to my family too. Given the events of the year, I'm reminded to hold them all close. They mean the world to me.

Biggest thank you of all to every single one of my readers. I couldn't do this without you. Wishing everyone a very Merry Christmas.

Chris

xoxo

Also by Chris Reilly

The Devil's Chaos Duet:
Devil's Chaos
Devil's Daughter

Novellas:
Devil's Desire
Devil's Kiss

BreakNeck Series:
Sky Full of Stars
Touch in the Dark
The Sounds of Her
Perfect Storm

Spin-Off Novellas:
Standing Still
Fight For Forever

Sports Romance:
Off The Line

Red Alert Series:
Electric Touch
Midnight Heat

Standalone Romance:
Reckless
Christmas Eve, Eve

About the Author

I was born and raised in Liverpool, UK and loved to read from as early as I can remember. Writing came along when I was about 13-14 and English and essay writing (creative obviously) became my favorite lesson! I currently live with my son and our two new kittens, Archie and Ash, or Menace and Torment as they're more commonly known.

The majority of my 20's/30's I read thrillers. Both mysteries and detective-based books. I made the switch to romance when I picked up a book called 'Dirty Letters' I loved it and the authors so much, I went looking for more. I then went down the rabbit hole of Indie Romance and was amazed and inspired by these amazing authors and decided to put my writing "hobby" to the test.

Happily ever after is always the goal for my characters, but there may be a cliff-hanger or two, and definitely some angsty situations to work through, occasionally a little bit dark, but oh so delicious.